A DIRTY DOZEN Cl

The Dirty Dozen 7

Marla Monroe

MENAGE EVERLASTING

Siren Publishing, Inc.
www.SirenPublishing.com

A SIREN PUBLISHING BOOK
IMPRINT: Ménage Everlasting

A DIRTY DOZEN CHRISTMAS
Copyright © 2013 by Marla Monroe

ISBN: 978-1-62242-534-1

First Printing: February 2013

Cover design by Les Byerley
All art and logo copyright © 2013 by Siren Publishing, Inc.

Printed in the U.S.A.

PUBLISHER
Siren Publishing, Inc.
www.SirenPublishing.com

DEDICATION

This is for all of you out there who asked for another Dirty Dozen book.

A DIRTY DOZEN CHRISTMAS

The Dirty Dozen 7

MARLA MONROE
Copyright © 2013

Chapter One

"I think it's a brilliant idea, Parker!" Tina walked over to pour another round of margaritas from the blender.

She filled each glass before returning to the counter to mix up another batch. Once or twice a month, the Dirty Dozen families got together at someone's house to hang out and catch up on everyone's life. They had decided to get together this Saturday since Halloween actually fell on a Sunday this year. They always got together on Halloween. In years past, they had all gone to the costume party at the local bar, but this year they had children to think about. They decided to make it a family event instead.

This time it was at Tina, Cole, and Zack's place. Cole was the leader with Zack as his second-in-command for the gang. Their gang rode bikes and worked together in construction as a freelance type of crew under The Dirty Dozen Construction Company.

"What does everyone else think about the idea?" Tina asked after firing up the blender once again.

"I'm all for it. I'll be glad to help set it up, Parker." Alexis was Neal and Mark's wife.

"Count me in," Briana added.

"Me, too," Brandy said.

"You know I'm in." Carly grinned as she took a sip of the homemade concoction.

"So we're all in agreement? We're going to be a sponsor of the Dallas Children's Home this Christmas?" Tina brought the freshly made pitcher of drinks over to the table where everyone was sitting so it would be available when they wanted a refill.

"Absolutely. I think it will be fun to raise money and wrap gifts for them." Alexis cupped her hands around her glass.

"I'll get a complete list of each child and their information, like sizes and favorite colors to use when we get ready to go shopping. The first thing we need to do is make plans on what type of fund-raiser we want to do." Parker was Shane and Allen's wife and had connections in the social world.

Tina smiled at the women around the table. She loved being a part of such a fun-loving and caring group of women. They had a lot in common besides the fact that they were all married to members of The Dirty Dozen Construction Group. They each lived in a ménage relationship with their two husbands and knew what it was like to have to deal with prejudices and controversy.

She enjoyed their company and felt like they were all a part of her extended family. They had shared everything, both good and bad and survived. This Christmas they planned on celebrating together, and she couldn't wait. Parker's idea to sponsor the Dallas Children's Home this Christmas was more proof that she was part of the greatest family in the world.

The group had never sponsored a charity before. Though they had each donated their time and money to various things in the past, this was the first time they would be working together on something. It looked as if all of the women were excited about the idea.

"So what are the suggestions for fund-raisers?" Briana asked.

"I think a bake sale would be a good idea. If we do it at Thanksgiving, we could probably sell out of everything fairly quickly." Alexis got up and grabbed a pad and pencil to make notes with.

"How about a raffle?" Brandy suggested. "We'd have to come up with something that would create interest to raffle off, but they usually do well."

Tina thought both ideas were good ones. She looked over at Parker. The other woman was chewing her bottom lip with a thoughtful look on her face.

"What are you thinking so hard about over there, Parker?"

"How about raffling off a home improvement project? That would get some interest going, and it would get the men involved as well."

Tina popped her hand over her mouth before she burst out laughing. It was a brilliant idea. She exchanged glances with the other women and they all grinned at the same time.

"Well? What do you think?"

Parker had been the last to join their little group, and because of her wealthy connections she often worried that her background interfered with being accepted by everyone. No matter how much Tina tried to reassure her, Parker continued to worry.

"It's perfect! Getting the guys in on it is a great idea. We'll need to talk to them on how to describe the prize though. Just saying a home improvement project can mean just about anything." Tina wrapped her arms around Parker and hugged her. "You're amazing."

Parker blushed but didn't say anything. Tina had no doubt she would be in her element spearheading the entire process once they had everything figured out.

Briana sipped at her drink and waved her hand. "The guys are going to freak when they hear what we've signed them up for."

Alexis chuckled and nodded her head. "They've been lazy lately. It will do them good to have something to work on. What do you think, Brandy?"

"Kyle and West are driving me crazy being at home all the time." Brandy set her glass back on the table. "I send them out to take Matthew to the park, and that doesn't even keep them busy for long."

Carly glanced over at Tina and nodded. "I agree. The guys need a project. I'm only working part time now, and having them constantly underfoot is a pain in the ass."

"So who's going to tell them?" Parker asked.

Tina looked at everyone around the table and sighed. It would fall to her since she was Cole and Zack's wife and they were the gang's leaders. She would have to soften them up somehow to break it to them. She grinned. Somehow that didn't seem like much of a chore to her. She loved messing around with her men. They were gods in bed.

"Uh-oh. Someone is thinking about sex." Alexis wagged her finger at Tina from across the table.

"She's going to use sex to get them to agree to it." Carly just shook her head.

"Hey. We all need to be softening our men up for this. Just because Cole and Zack eventually agree doesn't mean your men will go along with it unless they think it will make you happy."

They all burst out laughing at the idea of a group effort at softening the men up. For the next few minutes they talked about how to advertise the raffle and bake sale and when to announce it.

"Well, first things first. We have to get the men on board and get the official description of the prize first." Parker interrupted their planning. "When do we all jump our men? I think we need to plan it to be the same night so no one finds out ahead of anyone else."

"Good point," Tina agreed. "Wouldn't work out if Drew and Ranger found out before I broached the subject with Cole and Zack.

"So how about we make plans for next weekend to jump the men?" Briana asked.

"Everyone on board with next weekend?" Tina sipped her drink and looked around the table.

Everyone nodded their head and grinned. Tina could already imagine some of the plans in her friends' heads. When it came to loving their men, they took things seriously. The guys in The Dirty Dozen took care of their women and treated them like queens. Nothing was too good for them. She thought about when she had first met Cole and Zack and how close they had become since then.

She had been a travel nurse riding her bike from job to job. When a serial killer had set his sights on her, Zack and Cole had promised to keep her safe. Despite thinking that she didn't want to settle down and give up her carefree days on the road, they fell in love and forged a relationship that she wouldn't give anything for. They filled that part of her that wanted to be loved for who she was without smothering her.

She still went on the occasional job with them to pacify that need inside of her for the open road at times, but for the most part, she was a stay-at-home wife now working the occasional shift at the local medical center there in Dallas.

A noise from the monitor in the middle of the table had everyone growing quiet to see if anything else erupted from it. Tina waited with them to see if the kids were waking up. It had only been about an hour since Matthew, Darla, Deanna, and Addison had all been put down for a nap. She hoped they would sleep for a little longer.

After a few long seconds, all remained quiet with the children so the women breathed out a sigh of relief and returned to making their plans. Tina eyed the monitor, wishing one of those adorable babies was hers. *One day, Tina. Take it one day at a time.*

* * * *

"Any idea what the women are up to?" Ranger asked Cole.

"Not a clue. Tina hasn't mentioned anything specific." Cole shrugged.

"Drew and I overheard Carly talking to someone on the phone this morning about making plans for Christmas. Carly making plans at all worries us." Ranger ran a hand over his head.

Zack chuckled and took a drink of his beer. "Tina can be a handful, too. She keeps me and Cole on our toes."

"Well, it's still two months 'til Christmas. We've got a while to figure out what they're up to." Ranger sighed.

"Have you asked anyone else?" Cole asked.

"Nope. Not yet."

Cole whistled and called all the guys over to where he, Zack, and Ranger were standing on the deck outside. He figured if one of the women was making plans, then all of them were probably in on it. It would be to all of their advantage to find out what they were cooking up.

"Hey, any of you hear anything about something the women are planning for Christmas?"

Neal and Mark shook their heads. Their wife, Alexis, was a paralegal and would probably be one of the ones planning whatever they were working on. Cole sighed. He had hoped they would have some inkling of what was going on.

"What about your wife, Shane, Allen?"

"Parker is always working on something, but I haven't heard of anything specific for Christmas yet. Do you want us to ask?" Drew stuck his hands in his pockets.

"Let's not stir them up yet. Just keep your ears open for now." Cole didn't want to act too nosey or he knew Tina would get miffed at them.

"You do realize that if Briana catches us trying to spy on her she'll have a fit." Dillon frowned at his brother, Gavin. "I was in the doghouse last time. It's your turn."

"I'm checking the calendar when we get home to see. I think it was me, not you." Gavin frowned at him.

"You keep a calendar of who is in trouble?" Kyle chuckled.

"You bet. That way one of us is always in her good graces to be sure she and the girls are taken care of. Otherwise, she'll try to do too much so she doesn't have to talk to us. When she's mad she tends to clam up and give us the cold shoulder until we manage to make it up to her," Dillon said.

"That's a damn good idea." Kyle poked West in the ribs. "We need to do something like that. God knows we stay in trouble."

Cole shook his head and laughed. The things they did to assure their wives were happy and content. He glanced at Zack and nodded. They would discuss that possibility later. When Tina got mad at them, she tended to go off and do her own thing without letting them know what she was doing. It gave them fits. Leave it to the twins to come up with the perfect plan.

"Hey, Cole. Do we have any jobs to do in the next couple of months?" Drew asked.

"No, I thought we could all use some time off since the holidays are coming up."

"Good. Ranger and I have a few things around the house we need to tackle. Carly has been hinting to us for a while now. I figure if we want to be in Santa's good graces we better get on them." Drew waggled his eyebrows.

"You mean Mrs. Santa, don't you, Drew?" Shane asked.

Everyone laughed. It was no secret that they all doted on their wives. Cole knew that each and every one of the men would do anything to make their women happy. It went without saying that they would all watch out for each other's wives as well.

He was proud of his friends. They had all served together overseas and had been through a lot. Although they had lost some friends along the way, the group had remained friends once they were all stateside and vowed to remain friends. When overseas, they learned about the ménage lifestyle and all of the benefits it offered. They decided once they returned to the States that they would build a ménage relationship when they found the woman of their dreams. Now, years later, they were all happily married and living the lifestyle they chose.

Cole stood back and watched his friends as they talked about everything from changing diapers to building hotels. His partner, Zack, handed him another beer.

"You know Tina has to be in the middle of whatever is going on."

"Yeah, I know. There is no telling what those women are cooking up. I have a feeling we're going to have to play a part in it one way or another. Either they will need us to do something for them or they'll need us to help them get out of something."

Zack chuckled. "Don't let Tina hear you say that. You'll be in the doghouse."

"I like that idea Dillon and Gavin have of keeping track of who was in trouble last. We can take turns and it doesn't always have to be me that she's pissed off about something." Cole grinned.

"Hey, it's not my fault you're the one who always loses his temper first."

"I think you've been conveniently overlooking things so you don't have to challenge her."

"It was working, too." Zack took a swallow of his beer. "Now that the calendar idea has come up, I'm all for taking turns."

Cole noticed West head inside. He bet the man had heard his son, Matthew, make a noise. How he and Kyle knew when their boy was awake even when they were in a different room, he couldn't figure out. It was like they had some sort of radar tuned in to little Matthew's frequency.

Sure enough, five minutes later West stepped out the door holding the six-month-old child and called for Kyle to get ready to go.

"We've had a good time, but it's getting late and Matthew is wide awake now. We better head home." West had Matthew wave *bye* to everyone before Kyle closed the door behind them.

Cole and Zack followed the rest of the men inside to round up their wives and children. It had been another welcomed get-together.

Now that it was drawing to an end, he couldn't wait to get his wife naked once they finished cleaning up. Zack caught his attention and Cole could tell by the look in his eyes that he had the same dirty thoughts circling around in his head. Knowing Tina, she'd be more than ready for a little family planning later.

They were ready to start a family and took every opportunity to put their plan in action. Even though it had only been about two months since they'd been birth control free, he could already feel Tina's desperation eating at her. He and Zack had their work cut out for them to keep her from worrying about it. In the meantime, they were more than willing to fill in the hours with some down-and-dirty sex. Thank goodness getting Tina in the mood wasn't an issue. Their lovely wife kept them hopping when it came to sex, and they loved every minute of it.

Chapter Two

Tina stretched after loading the last of the dishes in the dishwasher and switching it on. Zack and Cole had cleaned up the few things around the living room that needed to be done. The great thing about their friends was that everyone picked up after themselves, and cleanup afterward was always minimal.

A pair of arms wrapped around her waist, and Cole's unique scent filled her nose. She leaned back into his embrace.

"Did you have a good time, babe?" Cole asked.

"Had a great time. We all get along so well. I love visiting with all of them."

"The kids are growing up. Christmas this year is going to be fun with all of them."

"We probably better start getting gifts soon. We all decided that this year we're only getting gifts for the kids between the families."

Cole kissed her cheek and squeezed her tighter. "I think that's a good idea. We'll have so much more fun watching them."

"Who's having fun without me?" Zack walked in and kissed Tina on the cheek.

"We were talking about watching the kids open gifts this year. We decided to only do gifts for the children."

"It's going to be wild with the four of them wanting to tear into the paper. I bet we have an ocean of wrapping paper to clean up wherever we decide to have the group Christmas."

Tina stifled a yawn. She wasn't so much tired as sleepy. She had been up early that morning running errands before their get-together. She knew there wouldn't be any sleep in her near future though by the feel of the hard cock pressing against her ass. She wiggled her butt suggestively.

"Feels like someone is ready for bed."

"Oh, I don't know. The kitchen table looks pretty good right about now." Cole's soft chuckle sent chills down her spine.

"I've got her pants and underwear. You're in charge of her top and bra." Zack didn't waste time messing around. He had her slacks unfastened and slipping down he legs in no time.

Cole nipped at her jaw before he slid his hands underneath her sweater. The warmth from his hand against her bare skin was soothing. She hummed in appreciation as he sucked on her earlobe. She thought that by now she would be used to having two sets of hands and two mouths pleasuring her, but it still thrilled her. It still got her wet in mere seconds.

"Fuck, she's wet. Her cunt smells delicious." Zack hadn't bothered removing her shoes before he buried his face in her bare pussy.

Tina wasn't about to complain as long as he used his tongue on her like he was doing. It wouldn't be long before he would return to her clothes so he could get her naked though. She could wait until he got frustrated and took the time to pull them off so he could get her pants and thong down.

"Yes!" She reached back to wrap her arms around Cole's neck.

He had pushed her bra over her breasts and was pulling on her nipples now. Neither man had enough patience to completely undress her lately. She wasn't sure why unless it had something to do with their trying to get pregnant. Tina loved that they were as excited about starting a family as she was. It just made her love them even more.

"Fuck!" Zack had finally figured out he couldn't get her legs any wider with her pants around her ankles.

He quickly tugged her shoes off then helped her step out of her slacks and the thong. He stood up and shook his head at how Cole had her sweater and bra up around her neck. She just grinned at him as he finished pulling off her clothes, working around Cole's hands and mouth.

"I want her on the table." Zack pulled her away from Cole and lifted her to the table.

"This really isn't sanitary, Zack."

"I think you've told me that before." Zack helped her lie back before he settled himself in a chair and blew a warm breath across her pussy.

Cole attacked her breasts, pulling and rolling her nipples between his fingers before replacing one set of fingers with his mouth. He sucked her nipple tightly against the roof of his mouth, drawing on it as he continued to torment the other nipple with his hand.

Tina groaned as Zack spread her pussy lips and licked her slit from bottom to top before circling around her clit and starting over again. He used his tongue to tease, and he growled as he continued to lap up her juices. He never seemed to get tired of going down on her. He would lick and play with her poor pussy until she begged him to stop because she was getting too sensitive.

He let go of her pussy lips so that he could suck on them, cleaning them of her cream and driving her mad in the process. She bucked on the table in an effort to get him to work on her clit. Even knowing it was a lost cause, she couldn't help but try.

"Be still, Tina. I'll get to that pretty button in a minute. Let me finish my treat first."

Cole chuckled around the nipple he was sucking on in his mouth. The vibrations only added to the wonderful sensation of his teeth and tongue teasing her swollen bud. She arched her back in an effort to shove more of her breast into his mouth, but he wasn't going to let her lead in their seduction of her. Instead, he let go of her aching nipple and moved to her mouth. While his fingers continued tormenting her breasts, his lips caressed hers.

Their tongues slid against each other before he used his to explore and touch every part of her mouth. The teasing tangle soon had her gasping for breath. He stared into her eyes for a brief second then attacked her mouth once again.

Her attention bounced back and forth as first Zack then Cole pushed her arousal higher and higher. The constant stimulation of more than one place at once kept her climbing that tall mountain that promised the sweetest of pleasures once she made it to the top. The climb was almost as good as reaching the peak, but Tina couldn't resist the need to hurry it up. She needed to come, and her men were prolonging her torment despite her pleading for them to let her climax.

"It's too much. I need to come, Zack. Please!" She broke the kiss with Cole.

"Wait, baby. It will be so much better. I promise."

Cole nipped along her jaw then kissed and sucked on her neck and shoulder before returning once again to her breasts. Her nipples were sensitive from before and the nerves seemed to have a direct line straight to her clit. The more he played with them, the harder her clit grew until she felt it pulsating with each heartbeat.

"Look at that plump button. It's swollen and a bright cherry red. I bet all it would take is for me to lick it once and you'd explode. Isn't that right, baby?" Zack slowly inserted two fingers into her pussy and moved them around inside of her.

"Oh, God! Please, Zack. I'm begging you. Let me come."

Instead of answering her, he pumped his fingers in and out of her cunt several times before curling them and brushing across her sweet spot. She jerked against the table. He was right. All it would take was for him to lick across her clit once or put a little pressure on her G-spot, and she was sure she would come.

"She's begging, Zack. I say it's time. I'm hard as a fucking rock." Cole's voice was a welcome hum against her breast.

"I don't know what happened to your patience, but ever since we married her it sucks." Zack huffed out a breath.

"Zack!" She couldn't stand it anymore. Tina clawed at the table nearly crazy with need.

His masculine chuckle was all the warning she got before he latched onto her clit with his lips and sucked on the little bud while he stroked that special spot in her cunt. She felt Cole's teeth on one nipple while he pinched the other one. Combined, it was enough to send her flying. The sensations that tore through her body had her writhing on the table, thankful that Cole and Zack would make sure she didn't fall off.

"Your pussy is squeezing my fingers so nicely. I can't wait to get my cock inside that hot cunt." Zack slowly pulled out his fingers as she watched and sucked each one with a look of satisfaction on his face.

"Let's get her upstairs. I can't wait any longer," Cole said.

Tina suddenly found herself upside down over Zack's shoulder. She braced her hand on his hard ass to keep from bumping her head against him as he all but jogged up the stairs to their bedroom. She could see Cole's feet as he followed behind them. She couldn't help laughing all the way despite wanting their juicy cocks deep inside of her.

"What's so funny?" Zack popped her on the ass.

"Hey! What was that for?" she asked with a giggle.

"Because I could." He dropped her on the bed then started pulling off his clothes.

She watched both men beneath her lashes as they discarded one item of clothing after another until they were both standing in front of her totally nude. She licked her lips, wanting to taste their long, hard dicks. She crooked her finger to get them closer. Then she scooted to the edge of the bed and wrapped a hand around the base of each shaft.

"Fuck, yeah." Cole growled low in his throat when she bent over and ran her tongue all around the corona.

Without letting go of Cole, Tina licked at the drop of pre-cum pearling in the slit on Zack's cockhead and was rewarded with a hiss of breath his fingers digging in her scalp. She loved the feel of his barely restrained power as she lathed the soft skin stretched tightly over hard steel. Neither man tried to pull away from her as she moved between them, licking and sucking on their pulsing cocks. They rewarded her with small sips of cum until Cole finally gave in and pulled away from her.

"Zack, on the bed. I've got to get inside her tight ass before I shoot my load on the fucking bed."

Zack didn't waste time. In a matter of seconds, he had her straddling his hips with his penis pressed just inside her aching slit. He pushed upward while pulling her down with his hands on her waist. He speared her all the way to her womb in that one thrust. Tina gasped then moaned when he wiggled under her.

"Oh, God, Zack. It's so good."

Cole's hand gently pushed her down over his friend's chest so her ass was completely accessible to him. The feel of his shaft rubbing up and down in the crack of her ass sent a small electrical pulse straight to her clit. Soon he would be shoving his thick dick deep into her back hole. She couldn't wait.

For a brief moment, he moved away from her, and then the warmth of his body soaked into her as he dripped cold lube over her tiny rosette. The cool temperature had her squeezing her ass tighter. Cole swatted her butt.

"None of that. Relax, baby. I'll take real good care of you."

"Please, hurry, Cole. I need more."

Zack rubbed his hands up and down her arms and then her back as Cole began to press a lubed finger past the tight pucker. When it slipped through, he moved it in and out of her until he was satisfied that she was ready for more. Then he added a second finger and stretched her even more. Tina moaned, digging her fingers into Zack's shoulders.

"Easy, baby. Let me do all the work." Cole's sheathed cock pressed against her back hole. He'd added more lube, and she was afraid he'd slide away before he managed to breach her ass.

"Cole!" She called out as he slowly fucked himself in and out of her until he was buried balls deep in her hot, tight channel.

"Aw, fuck. Your ass is squeezing me so good. I'm never going to last." Cole started tunneling his thick meat in and out of her in long slow glides.

"Please. More."

Her cry was a soft keening noise as he slowly moved faster with Zack pushing in when he was pulling back. Then Zack pulled out and he pressed forward. Over and over they traded places in her body. Filling her and leaving her, gifting her with all of the pleasure she could handle. Zack's finger found her clit as Cole's gripped her hips. Their movements became less choreographed and more erratic with each plunge and retreat.

"Zack!" Cole's hoarse voice told her that he was close.

"I've got her." Zack's fingers moved harder against her swollen nub until she felt everything shift inside of her.

"Yes! Cole, Zack!" She spasmed around them, holding their cocks hostage to her orgasm.

In return, they erupted inside of her, their rigid dicks filling her body with their cum. Cole's hot spurts could even be felt through the condom as he jerked against her ass. Tina buried her face in Zack's chest as she screamed out the peak of her release. Every time with them felt like it was even better than the last time. It was if they stole her heart all over again.

Together they collapsed as one on the bed. Cole had managed to move them sideways though he remained deep inside her body as did Zack. She struggled to breathe around them. Nothing would get her to ask them to move. She loved having them tied to her for the short time it took for them to recover and move away to clean up. They returned a few seconds later with a warm bath cloth and removed the evidence of their lovemaking.

"God, I love you two." She smiled as they climbed back into bed and settled against her.

"We love you, too, baby." Cole kissed her, his lips sipping from hers before letting Zack have his turn.

"You're our rock, Tina. You keep us settled." Zack ran his knuckles down the side of her cheek.

Tina was right where she wanted to be. She needed them like she needed her next breath. They were the most important people in her life, and she tried to make sure they knew it every day. Their lifestyle wasn't always easy, but it was perfect for them.

Content and sated, she began to get drowsy. The conversations she'd had with the other wives of The Dirty Dozen floated back through her thoughts. They planned to seduce their men next Saturday night and broach the subject of doing the raffle for a room makeover as a prize. She thought about what she wanted to do to enlist their agreement and almost giggled out loud. Alerting them to the fact that she was up to something wasn't a good idea. They had ways to make her talk. She grinned. And she had ways to make them agree to anything she wanted.

Chapter Three

Parker watched as little Addison slept in the crib. From her head full of golden curls to her tiny feet, she was perfect in every way. Sometimes it amazed her that that beautiful little girl had come from inside of her. Then she reminded herself that Addison was a part of the love she and her men felt for each other. She was perfect because she hadn't stood a chance to be anything else.

She checked the baby monitor to be sure it was on before she turned to find her men. Tonight was the night she was going to seduce them into helping the women of The Dirty Dozen with their Christmas project. She knew the other women were planning their seductions as well. Although she was sure they would all agree to help without the sneakiness, it added to the fun of the project. Parker couldn't wait to get started.

Shane and Allen were watching TV in the den, so she had time to grab a quick shower so she would be fresh and ready for them when she lured them upstairs. She had already spent the day with her friends at the local spa. She'd been pampered, waxed, and buffed to within an inch of her life. All that was left now was the outfit.

She quickly dried off and applied her favorite lotion. Then she pulled on a black leather bustier followed by stockings and her black leather and lace thong. She had turned down the freshly made bed and checked to be sure everything was easily available on the bedside table. Making sure the baby monitor in their bedroom was on and working, Parker drew in a deep breath and checked her appearance in the mirror one last time. Satisfied that everything was ready, she slipped on her four-inch heels and eased down the stairs until she was within sight of the men.

They were still watching TV, each happily settled in their lounge chairs. She walked the rest of the way down the steps and sauntered into the den until she was standing in front of the TV. Both men lifted their eyebrows then looked at each other. Parker could see the questions in their eyes. Had they missed her birthday or some other special occasion? She would have laughed at their obvious confusion except she didn't want to ruin the moment.

Both men slowly got up out of their recliners and stepped toward her. The lust in their eyes wasn't hard to miss. Allen's light blue eyes had darkened with his arousal. Shane's dark eyes seemed deeper somehow. She shivered beneath their gazes as they looked her up and down before advancing on her.

"Baby, you look good enough to eat." Shane walked around her, trailing his fingers along her bare shoulders.

"I can't wait to taste her." Allen stepped in front of her and leaned down to kiss her.

His lips sipped at hers before he deepened the kiss to one that had her head spinning. His mouth devoured hers in an almost painful move. He slipped his tongue inside and tasted every nook and cranny. The taste of him had her head spinning. Maybe it was lack of oxygen instead. She didn't know which, but she had to cling to him to remain on her feet.

Then Shane's hot, hard body pressed in behind her, grounding her in the process. He sandwiched her between the two of them, effectively trapping her in their heated seduction. She had to remind herself that she was seducing them and not let them turn the tables on her.

"Let's move this upstairs." Shane's raspy voice betrayed how aroused he already was.

"Hell yeah." Allen picked her up and carried her up the stairs with Shane right behind them.

The moment they were in the bedroom, Allen lowered her feet to the floor. He kept one arm around her shoulders until she seemed steady on her feet. Then he trailed his fingers along her collarbone before following up with his lips and tongue. Parker shivered as he slowly licked his way up her neck to nip at her jaw.

Shane's naked body pressed against her back. She hadn't even realized he was undressing. The touch of his skin to hers heated her blood even as Allen continued his exploration of her neck and shoulders with his teeth and tongue.

"As much as I love this outfit, babe, it's got to go." Allen began unhooking the catches on the corset.

"The shoes stay." Shane's rough voice brooked no argument.

Parker stood between the two men as they slowly undressed her, trailing kisses down her body as they did. Soon she stood in her heels totally nude with both men staring at her through lust-filled eyes. Shane moved her back toward the bed as Allen began to undress. She found that she couldn't take her eyes off of him as he slowly pulled off his shirt, revealing broad muscular shoulders and a tight six-pack. Her hands ached to run over his exposed skin.

Just as Allen unfastened the first button of his jeans, Shane sat her down on the bed, breaking her line of vision. His knowing grin told her that he was well aware of what he had done. He pushed her down until she was lying across the bed with her legs hanging off the edge. Then he slowly went to his knees between them and shouldered them wider until he had access to her weeping pussy.

"You're soaked, baby. I can't wait to hear you scream when we make you come."

Shane placed a soft kiss against her heated sex before licking her slit from top to bottom. Parker gasped and arched off the bed at the decadent sensation. He sucked her pussy lips into his mouth and teased them with his tongue as he pulled on them. Then he was lapping at her slit as if he couldn't get enough of her.

Allen crawled up on the bed and attacked her breasts with his mouth and fingers. The added sensation of his fingers plucking at one hardened nipple while his tongue tasted the other notched up the arousal burning inside of her.

"God, it feels so good!"

Both men growled against her flesh as she fought to be still while they pleasured her. Shane sucked as much of one breast into his mouth as he could manage while he rolled the other nipple between thumb and forefinger. It was as if an invisible line connected her breasts to her pussy. One sensation fed the other until she thought she would explode from the slow buildup of tension deep in her core.

Allen thrust two fingers inside her cunt, pumping them slowly inside her. He twisted them and curled them until he located her sweet spot and then lightly stroked over it until she was thrashing on the bed. Both men used their hands to hold her down as they forced her to take the pleasure they were giving her.

"Please! I can't take it. Please let me come," Parker begged.

"Come for us, baby." Shane pinched one nipple then sucked hard on the other one.

Allen's fingers deep inside of her cunt pressed on that hot spot that always drove her over as he pulled on her clit. Heat swallowed her up as her climax washed over her, tossing her on an ocean of sensations that threatened to drown her. She screamed out their names as her body exploded in pleasure. Even as she drifted to shore long seconds later, she was aware of her men lying beside her, stroking her body and whispering how good she was, how much they loved her.

"Babe, I want that sweet mouth sucking my cock." Allen stroked her cheek with his fingers.

Parker smiled and rolled over on top of him. "I think I can manage that."

Allen grinned up at her. She lowered her mouth to his chest and began exploring with her tongue. She located one round disc and lapped at it until it was protruding and she could suck it into her mouth. Allen's hiss of breath let her know he was on board with her seduction. She moved to the other nipple and gave it the same attention. His hands clasped her sides, holding on to her as she nipped and kissed her way lower. The closer to his cock she got, the tighter his hands grew and the more noises he made.

She grinned as she closed in on his thick dick. He grasped her head now as if unable to help himself as he guided her to his throbbing shaft. Parker licked it from base to tip then slipped over and pulled the drop of pre-cum pearled at the top into her mouth.

"Fuck!"

Parker grinned as she savored his taste in her mouth. Then she licked all around the bulbous head before pulling his cockhead into her mouth and sucking on it. He hissed as his fingers massaged her scalp. The feel of his hands holding her head added fuel to the fire beginning to flame up inside of her once again.

She ran her tongue all around the underside of the crown then sucked him down fast and deep until he touched the back of her throat. His muffled curses were music to her ears. She loved hearing him lose control.

Just as she began to suck on him in slow rhythmic pulls, Shane moved behind her and ran his hands over her ass cheeks. She hummed her approval round Allen's dick, which had him moaning.

"I'm going to bury my cock in this tight pussy while you finish off Allen."

He popped her lightly on her ass then ran his tongue over the abused cheek. She hummed around Allen's shaft as she sucked him down to the back of her throat once again.

"Fuck, keep doing whatever you're doing. She's driving me crazy here." Allen's tight voice had her creaming.

"I can tell she likes it. Her pussy is soaked." Shane popped her ass once more then rained kisses over it before spreading her cheeks and running his tongue along her slit.

Parker felt him nudge her pussy with his cock before he slowly inched his way inside of her. She wanted to scream at him to stop playing around, but her mouth was full of Allen's shaft. She moaned around it when Shane finally pressed all the way inside of her. It felt so damn good to be filled by her men.

While Shane found his rhythm, stroking his dick in and out of her eager cunt, Allen began digging his nails into her scalp, letting her know that he was getting close. She redoubled her efforts in bringing him to his knees using every trick she could think of to make him come for her. By the sounds he was making, she could tell it was working. Over and over she swallowed around him when his rod was deep in her throat.

"Aw, hell, baby. I'm gonna come. Swallow it all." Allen managed to plunge deep into her throat two more times before filling her throat and mouth with his salty cum.

His shouting out her name filled her with pride and satisfaction. Knowing that she could pleasure him so that he lost control always made her feel like a queen. Then Shane began to shift his hips as he fucked her. Each move meant his cock touched a different spot inside of her. His hands gripped her hips as he pummeled her pussy, stroking over her G-spot with almost every plunge.

"Please, Shane. I need more! I'm so close. Please, please." Parker could feel her orgasm right on the edge, just out of reach.

Without saying anything, Shane sped up and began pounding into her as Allen moved to play with her breasts. Together the two men pushed her to the point of no return, and when Shane reached down and pressed against her clit, time stood still as she exploded into a thousand pieces and pleasure threatened to choke her. Every nerve ending in her body seemed to be alive with energy.

She heard Shane's hoarse shout as he filled her cunt with his seed, each heated blast adding to the overwhelming sensations traveling throughout her body. Finally Parker collapsed, trapping Allen's hands beneath her. When Shane followed, covering her sweaty back, Allen protested and pulled his hands free.

After a few seconds, Shane rolled off her and curled around her sated body. Allen disappeared briefly but returned with a warm wet cloth to clean her up. As they all three cuddled, Parker figured now was the time to ask her favor.

"Guys?"

"Hmm?" they both hummed.

"Would you be willing to donate your time to work on a project for me?"

Shane propped his head on his hand and smiled down at her. "I figured there was something going on when you wore those sexy heels."

"Yeah, I kind of thought the same thing." Allen kissed her cheek. "What did you have in mind, baby?"

"Well, the girls and I are going to sponsor the Dallas Children's Home for Christmas, and we need to raise money to buy their gifts." She ran her hand up and down Shane's chest as Allen rested his chin on her shoulder. "We were hoping you would donate your time to let us raffle off your services for a project."

"What sort of project?" Shane asked.

"Well, we would leave that up to you, but we need to know what you decide on so we can print up the raffle tickets. We were thinking along the lines of a remodel of a room or something."

"I bet that all the other girls are buttering up their husbands right about now, too. Would I be right?" Shane asked.

Parker smiled and nodded her head.

"Brilliant plan, baby." Allen kissed her shoulder. "I'm sure everyone will agree to work on it. We're not doing anything for the next few months anyway. As long as Cole and Zack are agreeable, it's fine with us. Right Shane?"

"Oh, I don't know. I'm thinking I might want to sweeten the pot some."

Parker furrowed her brows. "What do you mean?"

"Well, I was thinking that maybe you volunteer one night a week where we can do anything we want to you."

"You do that anyway." Parker laughed at him.

"Yeah, but I want to tie you up so that you can't stop us when we're pleasuring you. I want to hear you beg us to hurry up and make you come. I want to draw it out so long that when you finally do cream all over us, you pass out from how good it feels." Shane's face held such seriousness that Parker couldn't look away.

"It's a deal."

The monitor next to the bed suddenly let out a scream that let them know little Addison was awake and wanted some attention. The three of them grinned and hurried to dress. Parker wasn't surprised that Shane was the first to reach her. He loved his Addison. Allen held out his arms to take her from him, but Shane stuck his tongue out and carried her over to check her diaper. Parker rarely had to do anything with the men around.

Standing in the doorway, she watched as her husbands took care of their daughter and reminded herself again how lucky she was that they loved her. She wondered how the others were fairing with their plans. She couldn't wait to meet them the next day for lunch to discuss their success.

Shane looked up at her and winked. His usually serious expression was softened by the love for his daughter. Allen bumped him out of the way and took over dressing her before picking her up and bringing her to her mother. Parker hugged Addison to her shoulder and kissed her fat cheek before walking over to the rocking chair and settling down to rock her back asleep. Even as the little tike settled down, Parker thought about all of the children in the Dallas Children's Home that didn't have parents to love them and provide for them this Christmas. She hoped everything would work out so that they could make that Christmas one to remember.

Chapter Four

Alexis walked through the door of the little bistro where they were all meeting to discuss their success with Operation Seduction the night before. Everyone was already sitting around two tables that had been pushed together to accommodate their group. She smiled and waved as she walked over.

"Hey Alexis. How was your night?" Brandy's smile took up her entire face.

"Let's put it this way. I have some tender areas this morning."

Everyone giggled and nodded. She could see that they all had some tender spots of their own. She couldn't wait to get started on setting up the raffle.

"So? Is everyone on board?" she asked.

"Yep. We all were successful. Cole and Zack were going to get the guys together tonight when we get home to decide on what sort of project they would offer for the prize." Tina had a rosy glow to her face.

A waitress walked up and quickly took their orders. Alexis listened as everyone started back up again once the woman had finished and walked away to turn in their orders. They were all filled with excitement and she loved being a part of the group. Even though she still worked part time as a paralegal for a local law firm in Dallas, she no longer had the stress and anxiety that had caused her ulcers before. Now she could relax and enjoy herself without it being about work. Loving Neal and Mark was the best thing that had ever happened to her.

"So, let's make a list of what we are each going to bake for the bake sale. Parker has gotten permission for us to sell our food outside the grocery store near her house. We thought having the sale on the Tuesday before Thanksgiving would be a good day." Tina opened a notebook and wrote everyone's name down.

Brandy spoke up. "I'll make four pecan pies."

"I'll make a couple of different cakes," Carly added.

"Count me in for a German chocolate cake and a couple of sweet potato pies," Briana said.

Alexis added that she would bring bags of cookies. Once everyone had volunteered their baked goods, the waitress was back with their orders. They talked about planning a day to Christmas shop together for their families and then chose a day to shop for the kids. Parker made notes on her calendar as did Tina. She knew that between the two of them, they would remind the rest of them closer to time.

Parker's friend Sarah Beth breezed into the building and hurried over to where they were sitting. She looked upset.

"Hey, Sarah Beth." Parker stood up and hugged her before the other woman pulled up a chair and sat down next to her.

"We've got a problem," she said.

"What's up?" Parker frowned.

"I was out at the country club and overheard Caro talking to her friends about the Dallas Children's Home. She said that when she had called to tell them her group was going to sponsor them this year, she was told that another group had already volunteered. One of the women asked her who had gotten them. I could tell that Caro was furious by the color of her face. She told them that a group called The Dirty Dozen MC had volunteered."

"Damn. What happened then?" Parker asked.

"Elizabeth, Olivia's friend, knew who you were and immediately told them."

Tina laughed. "I bet that went over well."

"Um, I'm not sure I would say that." Sarah Beth bit her lower lip.

"Go on. Spill it." Parker frowned.

"She told them all about that you lived with two men and that they were a biker gang. She made it sound so dirty and dangerous. The other women were all up in arms and were talking about protesting to the children's home."

Parker sighed. "It won't matter. I talked with the board of directors for the home and they know all about us and what our husbands do. Two of the men on the board have had work done by The Dirty Dozen Construction Company before. I don't think there's anything to worry about."

"I hope you're right." Alexis wasn't so sure they wouldn't have problems. She knew how legalities could turn on you.

"There's nothing those women can do to usurp our place as the sponsors. I'm sure they're going to make some noise, but we can handle them." Parker shrugged. "Besides, I've been bored lately. This will give me something to work on. I'll keep my feelers out to see what they're up to."

Tina laughed. "Parker, honey, remember that we're all part of the group. We can help. Don't think that everything is on you to take care of."

Sarah Beth smiled. "Tina already knows you're going to try and shoulder all the responsibilities all alone. Let them help you for a change. I'll keep up with what Caro and her friends are working on."

Brandy leaned over toward Alexis and said, "I can't wait 'til we go shopping for the kids. That's going to be the most fun."

"Has Parker gotten a list of kids for us yet?" Brandy asked.

"Hey, Parker. Do you have a list of kids yet?" she asked.

"Not yet. I'll get the list when we get ready to go shopping. We don't want to leave out someone that shows up later. Most of the kids who live there are older, so I doubt any of them will be gone before Christmas, but they may get a new one or two in. Right now there are fifteen boys and girls there from about eleven to sixteen."

"I guess since they are older, they don't have as much of a chance at adoption as the little kids do." Briana's eyes glistened as she spoke.

"That's why I want to be sure we make this Christmas a good one for them," Tina said.

Alexis agreed. The thought of all those children growing up without a parent to love them broke her heart. She knew Mark and Neal felt the same way. They had talked about it before she had left to meet the other women for lunch. Children needed to feel loved and accepted. Growing up without someone to offer that had to be tough. She was sure the people who worked with them did their best, but it wasn't the same as having your own parents.

She listened in as the others discussed what had to be done to get ready for the bake sale. She and Briana were going to print the signs for the bake sale and the tickets for the raffle. Now that the date had been decided for the bake sale, she and Briana could start designing the signs and getting them ready to distribute.

"Any idea what the guys are going to want to do for the raffle yet?" she asked Tina.

"I don't have a clue. They said they would decide tonight and let us know."

Carly stood up and stretched. "I better run. I need to work on some laundry. I'll talk to you later."

Alexis stood up as the others began to do the same. She needed to think about getting ready for work the next day as well. She would be able to get more done once the guys had left to meet about the raffle project, but she hoped they would be up for a little fooling around in the meantime.

Just as she was pulling out of the parking lot, someone got out of a car and approached Parker. She almost pulled back in, but someone had pulled into her parking place so she continued down the road, heading for home. Something didn't seem right about what she had seen. As soon as she got home, she was going to call Parker and be sure the other woman was okay.

* * * *

Dillon and Gavin walked into Fugly's bar at 6:00 p.m. and headed straight to where the others had gathered in the back around several tables. Gavin nodded at the others as he and Dillon took their seats. He could tell the conversation was about Parker from the expressions on everyone's face.

"So this bitch saw her car and stopped just to attack her?" Ranger was asking.

Allen nodded. "She was yelling at her before she even got out of the car good. Called her a slut and a whore. I swear if she wasn't a woman I'd teach her a lesson."

"What did Parker do?" Kyle asked.

Shane smiled evilly. "She laughed and told her she was just jealous because she couldn't get one man of her own, much less two."

"So what is it all about? Why did this start back up?" Neal asked.

"It seems that another women's group had decided to sponsor the children's orphanage our women are sponsoring, and when they found out who had beat them to the punch, they decided to be pissy about it." Cole took a pull on his beer.

Gavin didn't like the sound of things. He didn't want Briana to have to deal with shit like that. He didn't have a clue what they could do about it though. He and Dillon exchanged glances.

"Maybe they should think about backing away from this one and choose something else," he finally said.

"Are you going to be the one to suggest that to them?" Zack shook his head.

Gavin sighed. "I see your point. Briana would cut us off for even thinking about it."

"Tina has her heart set on helping those kids. I don't think there's any way they'll back away from this," Cole said.

"Then I guess we better come up with a project for them to raffle off," West said.

"What are the suggestions, guys?" Zack had a pad and pen ready to make notes.

They batted around several ideas from an elaborate deck to designing a home office complete with custom-built shelves and a built-in desk. They talked about the pros and cons of each idea and quickly dismissed the deck since they would be doing the work during the months of January and February. They would need to be able to work inside as much as possible with the weather being cold and possibly wet.

"I like the idea of the home office," Ranger said, "but a library would be nice, too."

"If we narrow it down to one thing, it might cut out a lot of potential sales with people who don't need a library or an office. Why don't we list an offer to make over any single room except a bathroom or bedroom?" Kyle suggested.

"I think Kyle's right, but I think we need to list what we'll do so there's no unexpected demands." Allen exchanged his empty bottle for a fresh beer from the waitress.

"Good point," Cole said.

Zack was busy making notes. Gavin watched the other man, noting that he seemed worried. He kept looking at his watch. Come to think of it, Cole seemed preoccupied as well. Where they worried about Tina for some reason?

They all talked over the various ideas for several more minutes before everyone finally agreed to list three projects the winner could choose from. Zack pulled out his cell phone and texted someone then nodded at Cole.

"Okay, it's settled then. We'll list the three projects as custom-built cabinets in the kitchen, custom-built desk and shelves in an office, or custom shelves and cabinets in a laundry room." Cole stood up. "Okay, guys. That settles everything. Zack and I need to get home. We'll talk to you later."

The group broke up and paid their tabs before heading out as well. Gavin glanced over at Dillon as they climbed into the truck. His brother must have caught on to Zack and Cole's preoccupation with something else.

"What do you think is going on with them?" Dillon asked as they pulled out of the parking lot.

"I'm not sure. Did you see Zack text someone several times?"

"Bet it was Tina. I bet they're worried about how all of this is affecting her. I know I'm not too thrilled with Briana dealing with a bunch of bitchy women."

"Yeah, but I know I'm not about to tell her she doesn't need to get involved." Gavin steered toward home.

"Maybe it will cool off now pretty quick. Now that it's a done deal with the children's home, they will probably find another charity to work on and forget about it."

Gavin wasn't so sure about that. He had a bad feeling about everything. He couldn't help but feel relieved when they pulled into their drive several minutes later. As soon as they walked into the door, he headed for the nursery to check on Darla and Deanna. Both girls were sound asleep. He smiled to himself. They were beautiful as they lay sleeping. Lord knew they were a handful when awake.

He turned to walk out of the room and almost ran over his brother. The other man grinned at him.

"Hard to believe they are so quiet, isn't it."

"Shhh, don't wake them up." Gavin shook his head and slapped Gavin on the shoulder. "Where's Briana?"

"Sound asleep in her chair with her Kindle in her lap."

He nodded. "Does it look like she's had her bath yet?"

Dillon shook his head. "She's still wearing her jeans and shirt from earlier. I'll run the bath."

Gavin followed Dillon to the bedroom where sure enough, Briana was stretched out in her lounge chair with her e-reader. He wondered what she had been reading before she fell asleep. Probably one of her sexy books, as he called them. He loved it when she had been reading one of them and came to get them. She was always so hot and wet for them. After their round of raunchy sex the night before, he knew she would be a little sore. A nice hot bath would help her relax and sleep.

Dillon walked out of the bathroom. "Bath's ready. I'll help you undress her."

They walked over and knelt down beside her chair. Dillon bent over and kissed her lightly on the lips. Gavin kissed her neck and then nipped lightly at her jaw. Her eyes fluttered open, and a smile pulled at her lips.

"Hey, you're back." She sat up and stretched. "What did you all decide on?"

"We'll tell you all about it while you soak. Dillon has your bath ready." Gavin began unbuttoning her shirt.

"Mmm, that sounds good. Did you check on the girls? Are they still asleep?"

"Sound asleep, baby. Come on. Let's get these jeans off of you." Gavin helped her stand as Dillon pulled her shirt off.

"Didn't realize I was sleepy."

"Either that or your book wasn't very interesting." Dillon winked at her.

Briana's face turned a pretty shade of pink. She had been reading one of her dirty books. He couldn't help but tease her.

"So what was it tonight? BDSM or a little ménage?"

"Maybe it was just a normal book with normal sex."

"Honey, you don't do anything normal." Dillon chuckled.

Once again her face turned pink, but she pouted and marched toward the bathroom with them right behind her. He couldn't help but groan at the lovely view of her twitching ass as she walked ahead of them. He glanced over and caught Dillon adjusting his dick in his pants. Fuck that. He began tugging on his belt with the intentions of getting naked. He stopped to pull off his boots then hurried to the bathroom to claim his seat in the tub. It was no surprise to him that Dillon was right behind him.

"Hey! What are you guys doing? I don't remember inviting you to bathe with me." Briana stuck her hands on her hips and glared at them.

Gavin cupped her face in his hands. "Please, baby. We want to help you bathe."

She tried to hold her glare, but it didn't last long against their puppy dog faces. He and Dillon had learned to make them soon after they married her. She couldn't resist them when they appeared to beg. Gavin wouldn't admit to begging for anything in his life.

"Oh, okay. No funny business. Tell me what you decided on for the raffle. I'm dying to know. We have to make the tickets and the signs to advertise it."

Dillon helped her get in the tub as he settled down at the back where she could lean back against him. He snagged the bath cloth and soaped it up to wash her back.

His brother grabbed another one and began washing her feet, careful not to unbalance her so that she fell back in the process. He explained what they had all talked about then told her what they had settled on doing.

"That's a wonderful idea. I like that. We'll get more sales by giving them a choice. I can't wait to get started on the tickets and signs."

"Do you need us to help with them, baby?" Dillon continued to wash her legs, moving up to her thighs.

"Thanks, but Alexis is helping me with them. She'll come over one day next week when we both have free time. I can't wait to get started."

"Just don't overdo it working on this. You know how you get sometimes. This is supposed to be fun for you, not a job." Gavin didn't want her to wear herself out.

"I won't. I just hope those idiots in that other group don't cause problems for us. Parker was really upset about it earlier."

Gavin and Dillon looked at each other over her shoulder. She didn't seem to notice. He planned to hang around wherever she went from now on. He didn't want something like that happening to her.

"I wish I had still been there. I would have backed that bitch back into her car."

Gavin jerked. "I don't want you getting hurt, Briana. Promise us you be careful when you're out somewhere."

"I'll be fine, guys. Nothing's going to happen, anyway. They're all hot air. I can't imagine any of them getting their precious nails chipped by doing anything to us. Parker might be from money and have social connections, but she's nothing like those other women. They're cold and act like whiney leeches just looking for somewhere to latch on and suck you dry."

Gavin couldn't help but chuckle at her analogy. He couldn't agree with her more.

Chapter Five

Carly stretched once she was finished loading her baked goods into the car. Drew closed the door for her and pulled her into a hug.

"Don't forget. We're all taking turns staying with you girls while you work your bake sale. If you need anything, ask one of the guys. There's no need for any of you women to do anything other than sell those cakes and pies."

She grinned up at him then kissed him lightly on the lips. Ranger pulled her his way next. He didn't say anything, just took her mouth in a hard kiss that turned her on. His heavy-lidded eyes told her he wasn't unaffected by the kiss either. She giggled and pulled away.

"None of that, Ranger. I have to get going. We can discuss that look when I get back."

"Can't blame me for trying." Ranger grinned and helped her into the car before closing the door behind her.

She quickly fastened her seat belt and started the car. She needed to hurry so she wouldn't be late. Hopefully they would sell everything quickly. She couldn't wait to get back to her men.

When she pulled up outside the grocery store where tables where already set up, Neal and Mark, Alex's husbands walked over and began unloading her car before she even got out.

"I've got your car, Carly. You can help the others set up." Mark opened her car door and helped her out.

Then he got in and drove it over to the side of the building where she assumed he was parking it. She liked having valet service. Everyone had already arrived, and the tables were full of pies, cakes, and cookies.

"Man, it's actually cold out here. I hope it warms up some." She was wearing a coat and had gloves in her pocket if she needed them.

"We've got a few blankets if we get too cold." Parker pointed to them lying on one of the chairs.

"The posters turned out great, you guys!" Carly walked around the table and hugged everyone.

"Yeah, Briana and Alexis did wonderful jobs with them. Don't forget to try and sell some raffle tickets while we're here." Parker pulled her tickets out of her coat pocket.

They chatted about what they were planning for Thanksgiving dinner on Thursday. They were all getting together on Saturday for a group meal. They started getting busy around lunchtime and were steady after that. The men took turns staying with them to be sure they had help if they needed it. The women took turns standing by the table and sitting in the chairs.

By four that afternoon they only had a few cakes and pies left when a group of women approached the tables from the parking lots. There looked to be about eight of them. Carly was sitting down at the time and heard Parker, who was sitting next to her, curse. Then the other woman stood up and walked up to the table. Carly figured something was up and stood up to offer her support.

"I can't believe they let the likes of you sell anything out in front of their store." This came from a tall woman with long blonde hair. She crossed her arms and stared at them.

"Caro. What are you doing here?" Parker stared at the woman.

"Wondering how you managed to get the manager of the store to let you sell your dirty cakes and pies here. I know I wouldn't want to buy them considering where they came from."

The women behind Caro all murmured and nodded. Carly noticed that a small crowd had begun to form. She had no doubt they were wondering what was going on with so many women standing around.

"Caro, why don't you get on with your shopping and stop causing trouble." Parker glared at the other woman.

Carly was glad to see Cole and Zack stepping up to the tables. The women all noticed and took a step back. Well, everyone except for Caro, who all but hissed at the men.

"I can't believe anyone would buy something from you if they knew you were living in sin and with a gang of bikers. There's no telling what sort of diseases they have."

"Caro, you better be careful what you say. I would hate for you to get sued for slander." Alexis had a pad and paper along with her phone. "I'm taping what you say. I work for a group of lawyers. It would be really easy to write this up."

"You wouldn't dare!" Another woman stepped up from the crowd behind Caro.

Alexis chuckled. "Oh, but I would."

"It's not slander for telling the truth, and it's the truth that you all live with two men and they ride motorcycles."

Someone from the back of the gathering crowd yelled out. "So! My husband rides a motorcycle sometimes. I don't see anything wrong with that."

"Right," someone else called out.

Loud murmurs began to move around the crowd. Caro didn't look the least bit worried. Instead she looked over her shoulder at her followers and nodded toward the store. They strode off, having stirred up trouble like they had planned to do.

Carly was afraid that their bake sale had come to an end, but when someone stepped up and bought one of the remaining items on the table, she relaxed a little. Maybe Caro's plan had backfired on her. Several more people stepped up to buy after that. They even managed to sell quite a few raffle tickets.

Cole and Zack kept the crowd from blocking the entrance to the store so that management wouldn't get upset. By the time they had sold the last pie, everyone was exhausted. Carly was excited that she had almost sold all of her tickets already. They still had two weeks to go.

Ranger and Drew showed up to help take down the tables and help pack everyone up. Despite Caro's attempt to ruin their sale, they'd done well. Now they had enough money to buy the wrapping paper and other supplies they would need to wrap all of the gifts they would buy with the sales from the raffle tickets.

Once everything was cleaned up, the women all said good-bye and headed home. Drew rode with her in the car. She told him all about what had happened with Caro and her followers and how Alexis had put a stop to her.

"I'm sorry you had to deal with that, babe. Ranger and I don't like this at all."

"Drew, there are always going to be people who don't agree with how we live our lives. All we can do is ignore them and not let them upset us." She smiled over at him.

When they pulled up in the drive behind Ranger's truck, Carly sighed. She had enjoyed the bake sale for the most part, but she was glad to be home now. Her feet ached, and she had gotten cold standing around. Ranger helped her out of the car while Drew unlocked the door. The minute they were inside, the men converged on her. When Ranger's hand began tugging on her sweater, pulling it over her head, Carly had no doubt what was in store for her. She grinned and ran, anticipating what they would do to her once they finally caught her.

* * * *

Tina sighed as she stepped into the house. It was so quiet compared to Briana's, Brandy's, or Parker's. She knew she was longing for a child, but did everything have to make her think about it? Zack and Cole walked in after her, and the whole atmosphere changed. The very air seemed to become electrically charged with their energy. Her men were angry. Tina sighed.

"I don't like it, Cole. That woman is going to cause trouble. I can feel it." Zack closed the door behind them.

"There's nothing we can do about it right now, Zack. I agree. I don't trust her." Cole walked over to the refrigerator and pulled out a bottle of water. He tossed one to Zack then held one up for her.

Tina shook her head. He closed the door and opened his bottle. After taking a few pulls of the water, he sighed. She knew he was thinking about what could be done to remedy the situation. There wasn't anything he could do to fix it. They weren't going to back away from their charity, and the other women weren't going to stop causing trouble.

"I don't want Tina going anywhere alone while all of this is going on." Zack leaned back against the cabinets.

"Hey! I'm standing right here. I do have a say in these things." Tina crossed her arms and glared at the two men.

"Not where your safety is concerned. We've talked about this before, Tina."

"I'm not in any danger. These women are all talk and bluster. The worst thing that might happen is that they call us names. They're too good to engage in anything like fighting or hair pulling."

"Doesn't matter. I'm not going to leave you unprotected. Live with it." Zack pushed off from the cabinets and disappeared into the other room.

"Let him cool off, babe. It'll all be okay." Cole wrapped his arms around her and nuzzled her neck.

"You're trying to distract me with sex, aren't you."

"Is it working?"

"Maybe." Tina couldn't help but smile.

Cole backed her up against the bar and nibbled on her lips before slipping his tongue inside her mouth. He licked every inch inside before sucking on her tongue. His hands weren't still while he kissed her. They slipped beneath her sweater and massaged her back before one slipped between her waistband and skin to squeeze her ass cheek.

Tina moaned into his mouth as he rubbed his thick erection against her belly. There was no doubting what he had in mind. If only she could get Zack on board as well. She pushed back against Cole's hard cock and wrapped her arms around his neck. He deepened the kiss, nipping at her lower lip before thrusting his tongue in and out of her mouth. She didn't doubt for a second that she would have swollen lips when he finished with her.

"More," she managed to get out around nips.

"I'll give you more. Let's take this to the bedroom."

Cole growled then picked her up and carried her over his shoulder with one hand on her ass. As they passed through the den, Zack stood up from where he'd been sitting, flipping through channels on the TV. She caught a quick glance of his face as the anger slid into need, and he followed them to the bedroom.

As soon as they entered the room, she heard the door slam behind them and Cole dropped her on the bed. Tina bounced once and immediately crawled to the other side. She slid off the bed and grinned at the two men.

"Strip, Tina." Zack's deep voice sent shivers down her spine.

"What if I want you to strip first?"

"Do it, babe. Now." Cole walked around the end of the bed toward her.

Tina backed away until she felt Zack's hard body behind her. When had he crawled over the bed, and why hadn't she noticed? He gripped her waist and leaned down to whisper in her ear. His hot breath sent tingles along her skin.

"You're playing with fire."

Cole reached her and slid his hands under her shirt before pulling it upward. He bent down and nibbled her other earlobe before jerking her shirt over her head. Tossing it to the floor, he reached for the front closure of her bra even as Zack's hands reached lower to the button at her waistband. They quickly divulged her of the rest of her clothes before lowering her to the bed.

"Don't move, Tina." Cole's raspy voice made her smile. He was hot and hard for her. Just the way she liked him.

One glance at Zack proved he was in no better shape. He jerked his shirt over his head with one hand and unfastened his jeans with the other without dropping his gaze from her. Nothing turned her on more than for her men to lose control with their need for her. She reclined on her elbows and slowly spread her legs wide so that they could see her wet pussy. She dipped one hand down her belly, pausing to flick her belly ring before drifting lower to slide one finger between her southern lips.

"Fuck!" Cole hissed out before he leaned down to nip at her pelvis.

He nudged her hand aside and kissed the tiny tattoo of wings before slipping to his knees and licking her fingers where they parted her nether lips. She moved her finger lightly over her clit before letting Zack pull her hand away from her aching cunt to slip her wet finger into his mouth. She sighed at the feel of his tongue wrapping around her digit, sucking the juices from it.

"You taste like heaven." His eyes darkened as he knelt on the bed next to her. "I'm going to taste these sweet tits next."

Tina felt her nipples pebble at the promise in his voice. Before she could say anything, Cole sucked her pussy lips into his mouth, taking away all ability to form a coherent word. He slowly released them before his fingers spread them wide so that he could delve deeper inside of her. She moaned and lifted her pelvis to meet him.

Zack pressed one hand against her belly so that she couldn't move. Then he lowered his head and nipped one nipple with his teeth. She hissed out a breath as he sucked the injured flesh between his lips and licked at it.

"Please! I need more." She loved having her breasts played with, but she wanted to feel them inside of her.

"Soon, baby." Zack released the tortured nipple and moved over to the other one.

As his wet lips closed over the little nub, Cole began lapping at her juices in earnest, humming his approval against her pussy. She didn't think she could take much more. Need burned through her blood. Even as she whimpered her frustration, Cole's teeth captured her clit and his tongue began licking over the swollen nub. She felt the sparks of her orgasm begin to build, and when Zack pinched both of her nipples at the same time, she screamed out her climax. Her fingers closed around Cole's hair even as he began to move upward to cover her body with his own.

"I can't get enough of you. I need to feel your hot cunt around my cock."

"Take me, Cole. I need you." Tina hated the breathy quality of her voice, but she couldn't control it.

Then Cole's cock slipped into her pussy with one quick plunge. The tightness thrilled her even as her body struggled to adjust to his girth. Nothing felt as good as Cole or Zack's cock deep inside of her. He pulled out then thrust back in. Over and over he shafted his dick deep inside of her until she was wild with the feel of him rasping over sensitive tissues. Her orgasm began to build again. It burned deep in her cunt and spread tendrils throughout her body. Her nipples ached and her fingers tingled.

"God, you're so tight. I can feel you milking my cock already."

Tina's fingers dug into his shoulders as he buried himself deep inside of her over and over. Her climax boiled in her blood, catching her off guard when it poured over her like thick, hot molasses. She screamed his name as he jackhammered into her then poured his seed deep inside of her. His cum burned against her womb.

Long seconds later, she felt her body begin to relax beneath Cole's. He slowly pulled from her and kissed her lips then her eyes as he moved off of her. She gasped for breath for several minutes as he cuddled her next to him.

Zack's fingers splayed across her abdomen in a soothing stroke. As soon as her breathing returned to normal though, he rolled over her and sucked on her breast. Moving from one to the other, he soon had her nipples plump and protruding like ripe berries. Tina felt the connection to her clit as it began to tingle and swell once again. She dug her fingers into Zack's hair and massaged his scalp until he released the nipple in his mouth and claimed hers with a deep kiss.

When he pulled away, her mouth chased his but stopped as the head of his dick pressed against her still swollen pussy. She hissed out a *yes* as he slowly entered her, inch by delicious inch. When he was fully sheathed within her desperate cunt, Zack growled and pulled back out. He treated her to the slow torture for several seconds then rammed his cock all the way to her cervix, bumping the tender tissue and sending shards of pleasure/pain all over her cunt. Tina's eyes rolled back at the feel of his hot shaft stroking in and out of her.

Fingers began to tease and pull on her nipples, and she opened her eyes to stare over at Cole. He grinned at her with half-closed lids as he tweaked and pinched her tight nubs. Then Zack began to pound into her body in earnest as if racing to a finish line. When she looked up into his face, eyes as dark as night stared back down at her. His mouth was slightly open and tight with concentration as he powered in and out of her.

"It feels so good, Zack. More." She begged with her eyes even as he grunted and pulled one of her legs up over his arm and leaned into her.

His cock bumped her cervix with every thrust now. She reveled in the sensations that spread throughout her body. She loved how he took her with such abandon. Flickers of pleasure began to gather as her orgasm swelled. It was like every time was the first time when they made love. Fucking her men bound them closer and closer every time. She couldn't get enough of them and thank God, they couldn't get enough of her either.

Fire erupted and sparked an answering burn in her blood. It flowed throughout her body and ignited all of her nerve endings as she let the climax overwhelm her and carry her wherever it wanted to.

Zack's name on her lips was drowned out by his roar of completion as he filled her with his cum. He stroked into her three more times before he finally collapsed and covered her with his body. Even though he was heavy, she welcomed the weight of him. It grounded her when she was sure she might fly away.

"I love you, baby." His whispered words had her heart stuttering. Hearing him say those words always thrilled her.

"I love you, too."

Chapter Six

Briana sighed and leaned back from where she'd been stretched over the computer all morning. The website was finally finished. She'd worked hard on it for the last week, wanting to have it done before Thanksgiving so they had time to sell some tickets through it. She smiled. Picking up her cell, she scrolled through her contacts and selected Parker's number. The phone quickly dialed her friend's number.

"Hello?" Parker's cultured voice made her smile.

"It's Briana. How are you doing? How is Addison?"

"Hey, Bri. I'm fine. Addison is playing in her crib. What's up?"

"I finished the website. Want to go have a look and tell me what you think?" Briana squirmed as she heard her friend moving around.

"I'm turning on my computer now. I'm sure it's going to be perfect. You're a genius, Bri."

"I just hope we can manage to sell some tickets through it."

"I'm sure we will. Hold on. It's coming up."

Briana waited impatiently for her friend to say something. She was anxious for everyone to like it. The site was designed to help with their charities. They planned to continue supporting their favorite charities throughout the year and use the site to promote them.

"Wow! Briana, it's fabulous. I'm impressed. Wait 'til the other girls see it. I'm going to call everyone right now." Parker's excited voice was all she needed to hear to relax.

"Thanks. I was hoping it would be okay. I wanted it to be classy but also reflect who we are."

"Well, you've captured it perfectly. We'll have to monitor how many hits we get. It will be fun to watch the count go up."

"I've got a stat program attached to it so we can see where all we are getting hits from and how many are new and how many have been there before. That sort of thing."

"Perfect. How's everything going for Thanksgiving?"

"I've got everything ready to go. I can't wait for Saturday." Briana was excited about the gang's family Thanksgiving party they were having over at Parker's.

Seeing everyone together and being able to just be normal was wonderful. There was nothing like having good friends, and The Dirty Dozen was that in spades. In fact, it was more like having an extended family than just a bunch of friends.

"Hug the twins for me. I'm calling the others now."

Briana say good-bye and ended the call. Then she got up and headed for the twin's room. They were playing in their playpen and seemed to be having a ball. She loved watching them communicate with each other as if they spoke a foreign language she didn't understand. When she walked all the way into the room, they both looked up and held up their hands. She laughed and reached down and picked up Darla first. Giving her a loud smooch, she sat her back down and took Deanna into her arms next. The little stinker grabbed her nose and pulled.

"You are both the best things in my life." She sat her next to her sister and stood up only to back into a solid wall of muscle.

"I thought I was the best thing in your life."

Briana smiled and leaned back against Dillon. "You and Gavin are the next most important thing in my life. Sorry, handsome. The girls come first."

"I guess I can stand to be second place to them. They are the most beautiful girls in the world." He nipped at her earlobe.

"Where's Gavin?"

"In the den sound asleep in his recliner. Want to fool around?" He sucked on her neck right behind her ear.

Shivers ran down her spine. He knew all of her sensitive spots. She turned around in his arms and wrapped hers around his neck.

"Fool around, huh. Sounds like fun. Think we can manage to be quiet enough he won't wake up?"

Dillon snorted. "I doubt you can. You make more noise than the twins do when they're hungry."

She slapped his shoulder and frowned up at him. "I do not."

"Let's go test it out and see." He grabbed one of her hands and pulled her behind him as he walked out of the twin's room and into their bedroom next door.

She smiled at him when he began unbuttoning her blouse. His dark gray eyes twinkled with humor. She loved how he was so fun to be around and his brother was serious and intense. Their differences made it easy for her to tell them apart. The way they moved and their scents were even different.

"So how's the website going?" He rested his hands on the soft mounds of her breasts once he'd removed her blouse.

"I finished it this morning. Parker said she loved it. I hope the others like it, too."

"They'll love it, I'm sure. No one can do better than you when it comes to web design."

"You're biased, Dillon." She laughed despite his frown as she pulled his shirt over his head.

"Don't argue with me, Bri. I know perfection when I see it, and you're perfect in every way." He bent and locked his lips with hers.

She hummed her contentment as he slid his tongue inside her mouth and conquered every nook and cranny before sucking on hers. She pulled back gasping for breath and licked her way down his chest. Stopping to tease one rounded disc with her teeth, she scraped the other one with her nails. His hiss of breath egged her on until she had licked and nipped her way down his torso until she was on her knees in front of him.

Looking up, Briana slowly unfastened his jeans and lowered the zipper, making sure to be careful of his rigid shaft poking against the material. Once she had it unzipped, his rock-hard cock sprang out into her waiting hands. Carefully, Briana lowered his jeans a little more so she had access to his heavy balls.

"You're driving me crazy here, Bri. Don't tease me." Dillon's tight voice thrilled her.

She dragged her tongue across the spongy head and tasted the salty pre-cum that had pearled in the slit. His breath shot out in a hiss when she stroked over the slit again. She loved the power she felt when she sucked them off. The feel of their hands on her head and the way their legs trembled beneath her hands had her pussy wet and throbbing in no time.

She sucked just the head of his dick into her mouth and ran her tongue all around the underside of the corona before backing off and licking the long stalk like a popsicle. She curled her fingers around his heavy balls and gently squeezed them before rolling them in her hand.

"Fuck! Bri. Suck my cock, baby. I need to feel your hot mouth on it."

She pulled back and looked up at him while she slowly took him into her mouth. She closed her eyes and hummed as she sank all the way down the velvety shaft. Dillon's fingers dug into her scalp as she swallowed around him then moved back up to tease him once again.

Dillon let her play a little longer, and then he took over, holding her head as he fucked her mouth with his steel-hard dick. She held on to his thighs, feeling them bunch with his effort to remain in control. When she knew he was about to explode, she reached around and sank her fingers into his ass cheeks, marveling at how they contracted with the first spasm of his release. Long jets of cum filled her mouth and throat. She struggled to swallow it all as he yelled out her name.

When he had finished, he slowly pulled from her mouth and went to his knees to hold her against him. She wrapped her arms around his waist and held on. When he pulled back and covered her mouth with his, Briana sighed in contentment.

"I want some of that." Gavin's deep voice made her grin.

"Brother, you won't last five minutes when she gets her mouth on your cock." Dillon pulled back and grinned up at the other man.

"See, you're the one who woke him up this time. Not me." Brianna gave him her haughtiest look.

"We'll see who makes the most noise, vixen." Dillon stood up and pulled her to her feet.

She glanced over to where Gavin was removing his clothes with a single determination. Dillon slipped the rest of the way out of his jeans as well. She smiled and backed away from them. No doubt they would soon have her screaming for relief before it was over with. She knew that despite her resolve not to, she would scream their names and scream loud.

* * * *

Ranger looked over Carly's shoulder at the website Briana had designed for the women. He was impressed. It was professional and informative. Still, he couldn't help but worry about their objectives. They wanted to support their favorite charities without hiding who they were. He knew from experience that there were people out there who would try and ridicule them. He just hoped that nothing more serious than snide comments cropped up. He wouldn't allow anyone to hurt his wife, much less any of the other women in their group.

"Isn't it amazing? She did a wonderful job." Carly gushed over the site.

"I have to admit she did a great job," Drew said from the other side of the desk.

"So how does someone buy a raffle ticket?" he asked.

"They click on this button and it takes them to a buy page where they select how many they want. Then they choose how they want to pay. See, they can use a credit card or PayPal. Isn't it great?" She grinned up at him.

"How do you get the ticket to them?" Drew asked.

"We mail the real one to them and e-mail their numbers to them. That way they know what the numbers are before they receive the ticket in case they buy one at the last minute."

"Sounds like you've got it all planned out." Ranger ruffled her hair before walking back into the den.

Even though they were doing all of this for charity, Ranger knew someone wouldn't care and only see that they were living with two men. They already had another woman's group up in arms about it. He hoped no one else with an axe to grind decided to protest their good intentions. He would hate to have to spill some blood, but he would for his wife and their friends.

"Ranger? Is everything okay?" Carly's sweet voice calmed him as nothing else could.

"Yeah, baby." He smiled at her and wrapped his arms around her as she burrowed against his chest.

"I don't think you're being honest with me, Ranger." Her greenish-brown eyes blinked up at him.

He sighed and kissed her forehead. "I'm just worried about how people are already reacting about you girls sponsoring the Dallas Children's Home. I worry about what might happen."

"Nothing's going to happen, silly. They're just a bunch of uptight snobs who are jealous of what we've got."

"What do we have, baby, that they're so jealous about?" He stared into her eyes, wanting to hear her say the words.

"We've got the three of us and we've got love. They don't have anything." She smiled up at him then rose on her tiptoes and kissed him.

His heart stuttered as it always did when she showed him her love for him. Years of feeling next to nothing hadn't prepared him for all of the love and emotion Carly could pull out of him. She was his everything, and he would do anything to make sure she was safe and happy. He looked over her head to see his best friend walk up behind her and smile. Drew's friendship had kept him sane before Carly. He couldn't imagine not sharing his love of Carly with him.

"I sent an e-mail to the others for you, Carly, telling them how much you like the site." Drew settled his hands on her shoulders.

Ranger nodded at his partner. He was always looking out for everyone. Carly leaned back and looked up at the other man.

"Thanks, Drew. I should have done that."

"You were worried about Ranger."

"He's worried about me." She giggled and reached down to grab both of their hands. "Let's go take a nap. I'm sort of sleepy."

Ranger chuckled. "That's code for she's horny."

"Yeah, I think I've figured that out by now." Drew wiggled his eyebrows at her as she led them upstairs to the bedroom.

Nearly an hour later, Carly lay sleeping between him and Drew with her head on his shoulder and her hand on his chest. Drew was draped over her back with his face buried against the back of her neck. Ranger couldn't settle. He had always had a sixth sense when trouble was near. His neck itched as if there was a sniper's gun aimed his way. Carly and the other women were in danger. He was sure of it, but he knew there was no way to convince them to back away.

He stroked Carly's head and kissed it. He'd just have to be on guard and make sure nothing happened to her or the others. He'd talk to Cole and Zack about it during the Thanksgiving party on Saturday. They would take him seriously. They always had.

Chapter Seven

Saturday morning Parker looked around the house and decided everything was ready for the party. The other members of The Dirty Dozen would be arriving within the next few minutes. She yelped when strong arms suddenly wrapped around her waist and pulled her back against an equally strong chest.

"You look good enough to eat." Allen's hot breath against her ear sent chills down her back.

"Promises, promises." She loved it when her men touched her.

"We're finished setting up the other playpen for the kids. Shane is moving the monitors into the office so we can hear them even if we're a little loud."

"Good idea. I think everything else is ready, too. They'll be here soon."

Allen kissed the spot behind her ear that always drove her crazy. "Too soon. I'd like nothing better than to taste test you right now."

She felt the answering heat in her pussy at his words. Nothing would have pleased her more than a bout of hot wild sex with her men. But, they had guests coming, so their plans would have to be put on hold.

Turning in his arms, she kissed him on the chin and winked. "Hold that thought. I guarantee they won't stay all night."

Shane walked into the den and grabbed her out of Allen's arms. He took her mouth in a searing kiss, molding his lips against hers and slipping his tongue deep inside to tease hers. Licking along every inch of her heated cavern, he mimicked with his tongue what he wanted to do to her with another part of his anatomy. When she finally moved back and looked up at him, she could see the barely controlled need deep in his nearly black eyes.

"I want you, too. Later, Shane. We'll have all the time in the world after they leave."

"Won't be soon enough. Maybe we can slip upstairs after we eat for a few minutes."

"Cool it, Shane. We aren't going to leave our guests at Thanksgiving to fool around." She chuckled at his frown and wrinkled brow.

"I bet Allen and I can change your mind." He nipped her jaw before kissing it.

"I would expect you to try. Just don't get your hopes up." She grinned and pulled away at the sound of the doorbell.

"Fucking parties." Shane's amused comment followed her over to the door.

Parker was struggling to keep her laughter at bay when she opened the door to Zack, Cole, and Tina. They were all smiling and carrying boxes containing food. She grabbed a box from Tina and handed it over to Allen to carry into the kitchen.

"Come in. I can't wait to see what you've brought." Parker led them into the kitchen where the men unloaded their boxes onto the counter before following Shane and Allen back into the den.

"Hope we're not late. Those two can't behave for five minutes." Tina looked a bit flustered.

Parker had a feeling she'd had the same issue with her men that Tina was having with hers, an overabundance of sexual energy. She couldn't help but wonder what that was all about.

The doorbell rang again, so for the next twenty minutes she was busy greeting the other members of the gang and arranging the food. By the time everyone had arrived, there was enough food to feed a battalion of soldiers. Everyone dug in to the buffet-style meal before settling down to eat. Conversation flowed easily between them as they gorged on all of the delicious food.

"I can't eat another thing." West leaned back in his chair and patted his stomach.

"There's plenty of desserts in the kitchen, everyone," Parker said.

"Better wait awhile. I'm too full." Gavin stood and picked up his plate.

Everyone agreed and they all helped clear the table. Tina and Alexis helped Parker deal with the dishes while Brandy and Briana covered up the food. Once everything had been taken care of, they joined the rest in the den. After a while the topic moved to the charity drive the women were working so hard on.

"We've manage to sell quite a few raffle tickets so far." Parker was pleased with everyone's progress.

"I'm looking forward to going to buy the gifts," Tina said.

"Do you have a list of the kids yet, Parker?" Alexis asked.

"Not yet. They've promised to give me one in a couple of weeks. They don't want to risk leaving out a new child or that we will buy for one that won't be there for Christmas." Parker squeezed between Shane and Allen to sit on the couch with them.

"I'm hoping we've heard the last from those nasty women from the other club. Just because they didn't sign up fast enough at the children's home isn't our fault." Carly sighed.

"I'm not worried about them. If they continue to cause problems, we'll just put them in their place." Tina shrugged.

"How do you plan to do that?" Briana asked.

"We'll take out an ad in the newspaper talking about it," Tina explained.

"I don't think that would be a good idea. You don't want them to try to sue you for libel." Cole squeezed her shoulders.

"Well we have to do something."

They continued to talk about the problem of the other women's group until time for everyone to leave. Parker didn't feel any better about the situation. She just knew the other women were going to try and screw up their plans. She knew them and had once been a member of their group. There were too many spiteful women in it.

Evidently Shane and Allen picked up on her mood because after they had everything cleaned up, the men began turning their attentions on her. Parker wasn't going to complain. With their having a child now, their alone time had been cut in half.

"How about a nice, hot, relaxing bath, babe?" Allen steered her upstairs to their bathroom.

Shane was right behind them. He wrapped his arms around her as Allen ran the water in the tub. Then both men slowly undressed her, dropping her clothes in the floor. Normally she would have protested and folded them up, but tonight, she was just going with the flow. She loved it when her men took care of her, and it was obvious that they planned on doing that.

Parker peeked at the bulges in their jeans indicating they were hard and ready for her. She wasn't going to waste the chance to make love when their daughter often interrupted their sex lives.

"That feels so good." She leaned back in Shane's arms as he rolled her nipples with his fingers.

"Let's get you in the tub, baby." Allen took her hand and guided her as she stepped into the massive whirlpool.

Both men knelt by it and began to bathe her, soaping her up first then rinsing her off. Parker felt like purring. They lost the cloths and began massaging her with their hands, paying special attention to her breasts and pussy.

"Aren't you two going to join me?"

"Not this time, baby. We want to take care of you first. We'll take a shower later," Allen said.

"Just relax and enjoy the bath, Parker," Shane said.

Parker sighed and let the warm water soak away her worries. It wasn't long before the water began to cool. Allen helped her out, and Shane had a large plush towel ready for her. They gently rubbed her dry then Allen picked her up and carried her to the bed. Shane quickly turned down the covers. Once they stood up again, her two men quickly removed their clothes, standing still for her to gaze on their drool-worthy physique.

It didn't take long for Parker to figure out that they planned to make her feel even better. Shane arranged her so that her legs were hanging off the bed while Allen knelt between her legs. He shouldered her thighs farther apart and leaned in to blow a cool breath around her pussy. Parker squirmed. Now that she was out of the tub, she was antsy and ready for some loving.

"I love smelling your arousal. It turns me on knowing you're hot and wet for us." Allen grinned up at her from between her legs.

Shane reclined on the bed with his head propped on his hand. His other hand was squeezing her breasts, massaging first one and then the other. She couldn't help the moan from escaping as they teased her unmercifully.

"Easy, baby. You know we're going to take care of you.

"Yeah, but you're going to kill me first," she complained.

Allen chuckled from between her legs as he leaned in and licked at her pussy lips. The simple touch of his tongue made her shudder all over. He must have liked seeing her do it because he continued doing it before finally he spread her so that he had better access to her. Then he sucked each side into his mouth before licking her slit from bottom to top.

Parker thrashed until he settled one arm across her pelvis to keep her still for his assault of her nether parts. All the time, Allen was sucking first one then the other nipple, swirling his tongue around the beaded nub. Between the two of them she was sure she would go insane. There was just too much sensation for her to handle. She could feel her temperature rising with their ministration. How long were they going to keep her on edge? She knew they might play with her all night from past experience, but she hoped they wouldn't chance that their baby would wake up and interrupt their fun.

"You taste so good. I could eat you for hours." Allen's hot breath flowed across her pussy.

"Please, Allen. I can't take much more. Fuck me."

"She's getting feisty, Allen," Shane said with a laugh.

"More like desperate," Allen returned.

"Please! Stop playing with me and make me come." Parker was half out of her mind with needing to climax.

Shane drew in her nipple and began to suck it tight against the roof of his mouth. At the same time, his fingers were pinching and pulling on the other one. It amped up the pleasure until she could feel her blood begin to boil. The heat spread throughout her entire body, building until she didn't think she could possibly survive intact.

Suddenly Allen sucked in her clit and teased it with the tip of his tongue. The more he sucked the higher she rose. Allen speared her with two fingers and began fucking her with them. It only made her wilder. Finally, as if they knew she couldn't take anymore, they gave her what she needed. Allen stroked her hot spot deep inside her cunt while sucking hard on her clit. Shane twisted and pinched her nipples.

That was all it took for Parker to soar higher than the mountains into an unforgettable climax. It seemed to go on and on until Shane let go of her clit and stood up to pick her legs off the bed. He moved them over his arms and positioned his thick cock at her opening. Without giving her a chance to recover, he plunged inside of her and filled her pussy with his dick.

She couldn't help it. Parker yelled out at the sudden invasion before moaning at the feeling of him deep inside of her. With her legs up like he had them, he was able to stroke deeper than usual. She was enjoying every plunge of his shaft as he pummeled her over and over.

"God, you are so fucking tight and hot, baby. I'm not going to last." Allen ground out the words as if he was in pain.

"Oh, God. Don't stop. Please, Allen."

Over and over he filled her cunt while Shane teased and tortured her nipples with his fingers and mouth. The combination sparked another climb that she knew would prove to be her undoing. Never had anyone given her such pleasure or shown her devotion like the two men she'd fallen in love with. Parker still had a hard time believing that they loved her. It was better than any dream she had dreamed as a young woman hoping for that fairy-tale life that women often wish for.

Allen continued pumping his dick inside her hot cunt, grunting as he did. She could tell by the serious expression on his face that he was close. Then he reached down and flicked a finger across her clit, taking her by surprise. Her orgasm jerked her over so quickly that she could only open her mouth in a silent scream of completion. Her pussy clamped down on his shaft, squeezing his seed from it, filling her womb with his cum.

Shane climbed up her body as soon as Allen rolled off of her to regain control of his breathing.

"Hope you're not too tired to take me, baby. I've been hard as steel all day waiting for a chance to fuck that hot cunt. You've been teasing us both since you got up this morning."

"Not true, Shane. I've only been teasing you since lunch." Parker smiled as he covered her with his body.

She loved the weight and feel of her men on top of her. Their warm bodies gave her comfort and reminded her that she wasn't alone. Gone was the Parker who had always felt cold inside. Here she was alive and a new woman that she not only felt comfortable being but one she could be proud of now because of all of her new friendships.

Shane positioned his dick at her entrance and rubbed it around in the combined pleasure of her cream and Allen's cum. Then he slipped inside of her. In one long stroke he filled her to overflowing. The spongy head of his cock brushed against her cervix with just enough power to send a light jolt through her body. It felt good. In fact, as he began to power in and out of her swollen folds, it felt damn good.

"God, you feel so good inside of me. I can never get enough of the way you both take care of me."

"Making love with you is heaven, baby." Shane's voice sounded strained as he continued to fuck her in long slow strokes that whispered across the sensitive spot inside of her.

It revved her up like one of her men's motorcycles. His hands were gripping her thighs as if his life depended on holding on to her. She loved it, loved the feel of him moving against her, the weight of him lying over her once he had climaxed and was still trying to capture his breath once again.

Suddenly Allen was back in the action, using his hands and fingers to twist and pull on her breasts. Her nipples stabbed out at his hands, aching for his attentions. He didn't disappoint her. He palmed them so that her spiked nipples pressed insistently against the palm of his hands. So focused on what Allen was doing to her breasts, Parker groaned when Shane slammed into her cervix with more force than before. The heat from it spread across her body.

"Please, please don't stop."

Shane's grip on her hips kept her from slamming into him as he thrust inside of her. She knew he was trying to make it last, but right then, Parker didn't care. She just wanted to come. It seemed like she was almost desperate to reach her climax for some reason.

"Fuck, baby. You're so damn hot and tight." Shane's breathe almost seemed to be pulled from him.

He reached between them and rubbed lightly over her tender clit twice, and she flew apart, free-falling through the burning lights behind her eyelids into a split second of total darkness. When Shane gently pulled his softening cock from her pussy, Parker opened her eyes and sighed.

"Damn!"

"You can say that again." Shane looked at Allen. "I swear the sex only gets better with time. It sure as hell gets hotter."

Allen chuckled, lying on his side with a hand stroking her abdomen in soothing circles. "I agree with you on that."

Parker stretched between the two men, noting the smug smiles they exchanged over her head. She hid her own smile, letting them believe they were the cat's meow. It was good for their egos, and a man was nothing without his ego. Even her two handsome hunks who treated her like a queen.

Chapter Eight

Brandy settled Matthew on her hip and closed the door of the car before slinging her massive bag over her other shoulder and heading to the restaurant where her friends were meeting. She shouldered her way through the door and immediately honed in to where the other women were waiting. They had gotten two tables pushed together and were chatting among themselves.

"Hey, Brandy. How's my favorite baby boy?" Tina stood up to take Matthew out of Brandy's arms to settle him on her lap.

"Great, you already have a high chair for him. Thanks." She draped the strap of her bag over the back of the chair and collapsed into it with a sigh.

"How is everyone doing?" she asked.

They all murmured that they were fine. She looked over where the twins were ensconced in their own high chairs. It was obvious that they had their own secret method of communication by the way they looked at each other and nodded or grinned. Brandy noticed that Parker hadn't brought Addison.

"Where's Addy?"

"She's fussy today for some reason, so the guys are keeping her at home."

"Poor thing. Matthew was like that last week. Hope she feels better soon." Brandy knew when the baby in the house wasn't happy, no one was.

"Okay, everyone. How are you doing with your ticket sales?" Parker got down to business.

They all chimed in on how many tickets they'd sold so far. Brandy thought they were doing pretty damn good from the sound of it. She was so proud of what they were doing.

Briana spoke up after a few seconds. "The website has produced over twenty ticket sales so far. I've already sent out the tickets and have the names and numbers stored in case they don't receive their tickets."

"You really outdid yourself on that website, Briana," Tina said, shifting Matthew in her lap.

"Well, we've only got another week before we need to cut this off and start shopping for the kids. I have the list now and am making a list of what we need to get, and then we'll brainstorm over the rest of the gifts." Parker waved the sheaf of papers in her hand.

Everyone murmured among themselves with excitement. They were all looking forward to doing the actual shopping. It would be fun to buy the toys for the kids. Briana smiled as Tina played with Matthew while carrying on a conversation with Carly. She knew that her friend wanted a child and had no doubt that Tina would make a wonderful mother. She hoped the other woman would get pregnant soon. It hurt to see the longing in her face.

A waitress come over and started taking their orders. Since Briana had been late getting there, the waitress took her drink order as well. She was very appreciative when the woman returned almost immediately with her iced tea. She was thirsty.

Just as they got their meals, the doors to the restaurant opened and the sound of several women talking grabbed her attention. Seeing who it was, Briana smothered a moan. The women from the other club who wanted to take their charity away from them. What were they doing there and how had they found out they were even meeting there?

She looked over toward where Tina and Parker sat across the table. Both women had noticed the other group as they made their way across the room. It looked like there was going to be another run-in with them women. She stiffened her spine and prepared herself for a fight.

"Caro, what are you doing here?" Parker didn't beat around the bush. Instead she took the bull by the horns and crossed her arms over her chest.

"I just came to give you a friendly warning. If you don't step back from the orphanage, you'll regret it."

"Are you threatening me?"

"Oh, not just you, Parker dear, but your whole little commune of sinful bastards. What you're doing is sickening. You have no business even being around those children." The other woman's face turned red with her anger.

"You have no say over what we do. Get a life and leave us alone. You don't want to tangle with me. You'll never win." Parker didn't raise her voice, but she sounded just as serious as the other woman.

"You haven't heard the last of us, Parker. Remember, I warned you."

"So Jillian? Are you really following around behind Caro like a sick little puppy? I never would have figured you for a prude considering your um, shall we say, unusual lifestyle."

Brandy could feel the chill in the air. Parker was obviously a force to be reckoned with in her world. She was glad she wasn't part of that area of the universe. She would take good old down-to-earth people over the snotty bunch standing in front of them anytime. Not that she would ever be invited into that group of people, considering her humble background.

"There's no need to be that way, Parker. I really don't care how you live your life, but the orphanage is ours," Jillian said.

"How do you figure that when we got there first? If you'd taken care of business to begin with, we wouldn't be having this issue. Besides, there are plenty of other needy charities that need support. Why not choose one of them? You adopted the women's shelter for the last two years. Why are you changing now?" Parker asked.

Brandy watched the other women and realized they looked uncomfortable. They obviously had something to hide. What was it? Her curiosity was piqued. Maybe they needed to do a little digging of their own. She would bring it up when the bitches were gone. It might prove to come in handy if they were really going to go for the throat.

"We just decided to make a change." Caro crossed her arms.

"Well, you should have made your decision to change a little sooner."

"This isn't over, Parker. You really should rethink your position on this."

Tina seemed to have had enough. She stood up and stared at the other woman. "Your threats aren't going to have any effect on what we do, so you might as well shut up and get out. You're not wanted here."

The other woman gasped and turned on her heel and stomped off with her entourage of puppy dogs following at her heels. Brandy couldn't help but giggle at the visual that gave her. Tina sat back down and sighed.

"She's going to make trouble for us. You realize that, don't you?" Tina rubbed a spot between her eyes.

"I know. I don't think there is anything we can do about it, though. We decided not to give in to her." Parker took a sip of her tea.

"They would have eventually caused trouble anyway. That Caro is a piece of work. She doesn't like us and has made it her mission in life to cause trouble." Alexis spoke up for the first time.

"Alexis is right," Carly said. "She has it out for us and the children's home issue is just a means to an end. I'm sure if we had stepped down, they would still have come after us."

"So what is our next move?" Parker asked.

"I have a feeling there isn't anything we can do to prevent whatever they are planning, but we can be prepared," Tina said.

"How do you prepare for something like this? You know they are going to attack our way of life. The thing is, we don't know how?"

Parker seemed to be blaming herself for whatever the other women were planning.

"Parker, you've said they were never your friends. Don't take on the responsibility as yours alone. We're all in this together." Brandy felt as if she needed to offer the other woman her support.

"Thanks. I can't help but feel responsible since if it wasn't for me, they never would have known about the rest of you. I tried to tell you all what it would be like."

Parker's expression tore at Brandy's heart. Somehow they had to weather this storm without any of them getting hurt. She wished there was something she could do to help. Tina changed the subject and everyone talked about Christmas and their plans. As they talked, an idea began to germinate in her mind. Maybe there was something she could do. As soon as she got back home she was going to be doing some research on the other woman's club. Something about the way they had shifted around when the discussion brought up the women's shelter charity had seemed off. She was willing to bet that there was something behind their odd behavior. She decided not to say anything until she had more information. There was no need to get anyone excited about it until she had something to show them.

Nearly an hour later, everyone prepared to leave. They gathered up their purses and Brandy claimed Matthew back from where Tina had him stashed in a high chair next to her. Again she caught the longing that crossed Tina's face before she hid it. Brandy pretended she didn't see anything as she accepted her son back.

After they had all said their good-byes in the parking lot, she buckled Matthew into his car seat and started the car to head home. All the way back home, Brandy knocked around ideas in her head and a sly smile widened her mouth. She couldn't wait to get to her computer.

* * * *

Parker pulled into the drive at the house and sighed. She hated that her past life was causing problems for her friends. She would never have called those other women her friends. They'd been causal acquaintances at best. She supposed even back then she had known they were enemies, but the better you know your enemy, the better off you were. Like someone said once, keep your friends close, but keep your enemies closer.

She finally opened the car door and stepped out of her vehicle. She wasn't surprised when Allen met her at the door. His dark eyes held his concern. How did he always know when she was upset? Did she make it that obvious? She would have to figure out how to alleviate his worry. She didn't like how all of her past was falling down around them, threatening to ruin their way of life.

"Hey, babe. You look upset. What happened?"

Shane walked up just as Allen closed the door. He looked from one to the other of them with a questioning expression. Parker sighed and taking both of their hands led them into the den where she sat down.

"How's Addison?" She wanted to know if her precious little girl was okay first.

"She's fine. She took a nice nap and is in her playpen right now. I have the monitor on me." Shane pointed to the mobile monitor on his hip.

"So what's going on, Parker?" Allen asked.

"Caro and her friends showed up at the restaurant and threatened us if we don't step back from the orphanage."

"How did they know where you were?" Shane's angry question mirrored her own.

"I don't know unless someone is following one of us. Either way we've got a problem. They are going to try to expose us and not in a good way." She wrung her hands.

"Easy, baby. Don't let them upset you like this. They aren't worth it." Allen rubbed a hand up and down her back in a soothing motion.

"It is my fault that they are focused on the group. Were it not for me they wouldn't even know the Dirty Dozen existed."

"Enough of this, Parker. I won't have you making yourself sick over it. No one in the gang will blame you for anything. We all agreed that you were a part of us and we would weather whatever came of it." Shane obviously wasn't going to put up with her self-flagellation.

Parker nodded and rested her head on his shoulder. She couldn't help but worry about how everything was going to end up. She knew Caro and her followers too well. They wouldn't think twice about the potential harm their actions could cause. All they cared about was themselves and what they wanted.

"You could use a nap, babe. Let's go upstairs and lie down." Allen stood up and pulled Parker to her feet.

"I'll watch Addison while y'all relax. She'll probably get fussy about being alone soon." Shane grinned up at them from his position on the couch. He pulled off the mobile monitor and set it on the coffee table.

"Thanks, Shane." She didn't know how she had ended up with two of the most understanding men in the world. They each knew exactly what she needed, sometimes even before she realized it.

Allen kissed her cheek and pulled her toward the stairs. Once inside their bedroom, she let him remove her clothes one item at a time. By the time she stood before him nude, her desire had edged out her worry. Her husband ran the back of his fingers over one distended nipple before she moved his hands aside so she could undress him next.

The feel of naked skin beneath her hands settled a part of her that was still uneasy about the fund-raiser and the orphanage. She slid the shirt off his shoulders before running her hand all across the wide expanse of his chest. Parker paid special attention to the flat discs of his nipples, scraping her nails lightly across them. She smiled when he shivered.

"Tease." He grinned and leaned in to kiss her on the lips.

The soft kiss could have turned deeper, but Parker wanted Allen naked. She brushed aside his hands as they started to wrap around her waist. Instead, she lowered the zipper to his jeans after thumbing open the button. The scent of man and sex teased her nose. He was as excited as she was. With deliberate care, she slowly lowered his jeans until they were caught at his boots.

"Damn!"

Allen chuckled. "I love that you always forget about our boots when you undress us. It proves how caught up you get while you're so horny."

Instead of saying anything, Parker shoved him so he sat down heavily on the bed. The slight bounce let her know he hadn't been expecting that. She made short work of untying his boot laces and pulling them off his feet before jerking his jeans the rest of the way down. Since he wasn't wearing underwear, she knew he'd been planning on a round of sexual excess even before she made it home. Sometimes she wondered how they knew her so well.

Allen interrupted her musings by pulling lightly on her nipple before she straddled his hips and leaned him back on the bed. She needed to feel in control right then. Allen didn't mind, as evidenced by his pulsing erection at her stomach. She leaned down and ran her tongue from one nipple to the next then sucked at them before moving to nip and lick at his chin and jaw. She settled her lips on the side of his neck to suck and kiss.

Backing off of him, Parker trailed her nails down his abdomen and then knelt between his feet off the side of the bed. She leaned over him, dragging her nails up his inner thighs until he shivered. She loved seeing his eyes shutter as he grew more and more affected by her actions. Knowing that she was the one who put that need in his eyes and the strain around his mouth gave her the ultimate thrill as a lover and her men's wife.

"Fuck, Parker. You're driving me crazy here.

She smiled and bent over him, licking across the top of his cockhead and capturing the pearled drop of cum that had beaded there with his arousal. His hiss was music to her ears. She dragged the flat of her tongue over the spongy head before running the tip of her tongue around the corona.

Allen tried to buck his hips in order to force more of his thick girth into her mouth, but she just pulled back and shook a finger at him. Then Parker took the entire length of him into her mouth and applied suction as she quickly backed off. It had the desired effect. He moaned and grabbed at her head.

"Easy, Allen. I'm going to take care of you. Don't I always?" she asked with a small purr.

"Yeah, but you tease the hell out of me first."

Parker smothered her chuckle and began to lap at his swollen cock in long, slow licks much like she would do if she were eating an all-day sucker. The more she licked, the more Allen pumped his hips having lost control of being still. She sucked him down again until he hit the back of her throat. Swallowing around him, she closed her eyes at the strained noises he made. Nothing turned her on like hearing her men moan and growl for her.

Patience gone, Parker set a moderate pace of fucking Allen with her mouth. He managed to keep his hands away from her for the first few plunges of her mouth down his cock, but after that, he threaded his hands through her hair and massaged her scalp in a rhythm along the same lines as his cock rising to meet her mouth.

"God! Baby, you're so freaking hot around me. Suck my dick, Parker."

She hummed around him and began to bob up and down on the long length of him. His groans only added to her own arousal and spurred her on. She slipped her hand between his legs and gently rolled his balls around in their heavy sac. She wanted to suck on them, but that would have to wait for another time. Right now she was too far along to be careful with them.

Allen began gripping her scalp with his nails, letting her know he was close as if she couldn't tell. His cock was already leaking small amounts of his cum, its taste exploding on her tongue. She lowered her head around him and swallowed hard. It was all it took to send him over the edge, filling her mouth with his essence. She swallowed his cum as fast as she could. Before she had even managed to lick him clean, Allen stood up and pulled her into his arms. When he had finished ravaging her mouth, he laid her back against the bed and took her place kneeling on the floor between her legs.

"I'm going to make you scream my name, baby."

Parker smiled. She had no doubt he would. When he lowered his mouth to her dripping pussy, she prayed she could hold out long enough to appreciate his expertise. Right now she was so close to coming that she was afraid one lick from his wicked tongue would set her off. Now that would be such a waste.

When she felt him clasp her hips in a tight grip, Parker knew she was in trouble. He wasn't going to allow her to slow things down. He was going to make her scream his name so fast she wouldn't know what hit her. She did the only thing she could think to do in the situation, she reached down and grabbed his hair in her hands and pulled him closer to her core so that he couldn't just tease her with his tongue. Now he had to give her a heavy lick that she hoped she could control.

"Might as well give up, Parker. I'm going to make you come so hard you see stars. Give me all of that sweet honey, baby."

She heard him, but she was too busy trying to hold on to her sanity to listen to him. It wasn't until he sucked her clit into his mouth between his teeth that a soft keening noise rose from her throat. Before long it had turned into a full-fledged scream of ecstasy with Allen's name on her lips.

Chapter Nine

Carly rushed home from work on Wednesday, so upset she almost ran a red light. They had known it was probably going to happen before long, but she hadn't expected it to be so personal. Anger warred with pain as she struggled to gain better control of herself before she got home and had to face her men. Ranger and Drew would be furious if they saw her so upset. They took making her happy seriously.

She slowed down as she entered their neighborhood and hoped she could keep her heart from beating out of her chest. Pulling into the drive, she was surprised when both men walked out the door to meet her at the car. Drew opened the door and helped her out.

"Are you okay, babe?" Ranger's gruff voice let her know he was already upset.

"How did you find out?" Carly let Drew draw her into the circle of his arms.

"Lisa called to give us a heads-up that you were headed home," Ranger said.

"Don't let it upset you so much, babe. It's what they want." Drew squeezed her tightly before releasing her so they could walk back inside.

"I'm trying not to, but they came to where I work and told everyone in the waiting room that I was a slut and a whore and they shouldn't want someone dirty like me to clean their teeth. My bosses are furious. They're going to fire me. I know they are." She sniffed, trying to keep the tears from falling.

"Shhh, baby. I'm sorry, but it doesn't matter if they do fire you. You don't have to work. You can do anything you want to do." Ranger smoothed his hand over her hair.

"I want to work, Ranger." She accepted the glass of water that Drew handed her.

"So, you'll find something else that suits you. Don't let them hurt you like this. They're narrow-minded bitches who need to have their asses spanked." Ranger kissed her cheek. "Now tell us exactly what happened. We'll need to call Cole and Zack about this."

Carly sighed and set down her glass. Then she climbed up on a barstool and turned to look at her men. They were her rocks and she knew they would support her no matter what. Damn it. She liked her job as a dental hygienist. She didn't want to do anything else.

"Caro and two other women from her group showed up and asked to see me. The secretary told them I was busy with a patient. The next thing I know, someone is yelling in the waiting room about sluts and whores. I walked in to find them telling the people there that we were living in sin by living with two men. She even talked about how some of us had children and they should be taken from us and raised by God-fearing families instead of being subjected to our depravity."

"So did they just run out of steam and leave on their own or did someone make them leave?" Drew asked.

"Lisa and I grabbed Caro by the arm on either side of her and forced her out the door. The others with her followed. Then as soon as they left, I told the secretary to cancel the rest of my patients and I came home. I was too upset to try and clean someone's teeth. I would have ended up hurting them."

"Well it's over for now. Why don't you go take a nice hot bath and relax? I'll call Cole and give him a heads-up. There's bound to be more where that came from." Ranger helped her off the stool and gave her a slight push toward the den and the stairs.

Carly couldn't fully shake the anxiety of what had happened. They were tearing apart her entire world. She loved her men and didn't want to lose them, but how could she live like this? Her work meant everything to her. They'd had this discussion before she had accepted them. She thought it was over, but here it was again.

While Drew ran her a warm bath, she peeled off her scrubs and followed him into the bathroom. He smiled at her and wrapped his arms around her.

"I know what you're thinking, love. You can't let them take away your happiness like that. They want to see you down and crushed. Don't give it to them."

"They're taking away my work. How am I supposed to feel?" She knew she was being a baby about it, but right then she could only think about the pain of losing something that meant so much to her.

"You have a right to be upset and feel hurt. I'm not saying you don't, but remember that you have two men who love and cherish you more than anything in this world. Nothing will ever take that away from you." Drew cupped her cheek in his hand.

"I love you, Drew." She felt ashamed of how she was letting this outweigh how lucky she was for having them.

"I love you, too, babe. Now get in the tub and relax. We'll have dinner ready for you by the time you get back down."

"I hope you aren't letting Ranger near the kitchen." Carly grinned up at him.

"I'm not that stupid. He'll set the table."

She let the water soothe her as she slipped down into the tub. He'd added some of her favorite bath salts and set out her towel on the heated towel bar. She was blessed to have Drew and Ranger. She could live without her job, but she couldn't live without her men. They were her everything. Not the job.

She wouldn't let those bitches take her happiness from her. She could be happy with her men without her damn job. She would figure out something else to do. Maybe she could do something from home like Briana. For the next twenty minutes, she soaked and let her mind wander. All sorts of ideas floated through her mind as she lay there.

Maybe she could learn how to do medical coding. She'd helped some in the office part of the business with dental forms. Surely it couldn't be that difficult to learn.

The water grew cold, so she climbed out of the tub and grabbed the warmed towel to dry off. She felt much better after having calmed down and thought through everything. The guys were right. She'd been allowing them to take away her happiness. They couldn't do that if she didn't let them.

When she made it downstairs, she found Ranger setting the table and Drew in the kitchen cooking. Ranger pulled her into his arms and looked down into her eyes. He didn't say anything, just stared. Then as if he was satisfied with what he saw, he kissed her and let her go. As she walked off, he popped her on the ass, eliciting a quick squeal from her.

"What was that for?"

"Because I wanted to." Ranger never gave a reason for anything.

She rolled her eyes at him and walked into the kitchen to find out what Drew was cooking. The tantalizing smell of lasagna met her as soon as she stepped in the doorway. He turned to smile at her when she hummed her approval of dinner.

"How long 'til it's ready?" Carly wrapped her arms around Drew's waist from behind.

"About twenty minutes. The bread is about ready to go in the oven." His hands rested on her hands. "Are you feeling better?"

"Yeah. I let them get the best of me and I shouldn't have. Like you said, they can't take anything away from me unless I let them. I'm not going to let them."

"That's my girl."

Carly felt Ranger step up behind her. He nuzzled her neck before kissing her cheek.

She was right where she wanted to be, between her men. There was nothing she would choose, even her job, over them. If those women wanted to fight, well Carly was ready.

* * * *

Tina waited while Cole and Zack talked to someone on the phone. From what they were saying, she knew it was about them, the women and the charity drive. She itched to pick up one of the other phones so she could hear for herself what was going on. Instead, she waited somewhat impatiently for them to hang up and fill her in.

Finally they finished the call and put down their phones. When Cole turned to her, she knew he was furious. Zack's face was closed down. She dreaded finding out now because she knew it would be bad.

"Cole?"

"It seems like Caro and some of her bitches have been busy today. First they went to the dentist office where Carly works and announced to the waiting room that she was living in sin with two men and that some of us had children and were raising them to be heathens."

"Damn."

"On top of that, they showed up at the lawyer's office where Alexis works part time and did the same thing. Fortunately her bosses were smart and threatened to sue them for harassment and a few other things. They left with their tales tucked after that."

"Poor Carly. She was already having trouble with her job. She's going to be devastated if they fire her over this. Alexis will probably be okay. I better go see about Carly." Tina turned to gather her purse and keys.

"Drew said she was doing fine. She's more angry now than anything." Cole dropped a hand on her shoulder.

"I need to call Parker and find out what we can do to stop this before it gets worse."

Cole and Zack exchanged glances before he nodded and kissed her cheek. "Everything will be okay."

"I know. I'm going to make sure it is." She pulled out her phone and walked toward the den so she could sit while she talked. She had been feeling tired lately.

Parker picked up on the second ring. "Hello?"

"Hey, Parker.

"I'm sure you're calling about Caro and her herd of cows."

"Yeah. So you've already heard. What can we do about them?"

"Carly called me, and then Alexis called after that. I'm at my wits' end about what to do about them. I never would have believed that they would go that far. I could see them whispering to some key folks but not this."

Tina could hear the tiredness in her friend's voice. She was sure Parker was taking all of it personally. She would feel like since they had come from her old life it was all on her.

"Parker, you know this isn't your fault. You know that don't you?"

"If it wasn't for me, none of this would be happening."

"Nonsense. You're not responsible for their actions. I don't want to hear any more of that kind of talk. Right now all we need to concentrate on is how to beat them at their own game."

She heard Parker's sigh across the phone. She could imagine how she was feeling right now.

"I'm not sure what we can do, but I'm not going to give up. There has to be something we can do."

Tina ran a hand through her hair and yanked at it in aggravation. "Well Saturday we are going shopping for the kids, so it's almost all over anyway. We'll go early and then have lunch together before we wrap it up that afternoon. Then we can spend Sunday wrapping the gifts."

"That's going to be so much fun. I refuse to let them take that away from us." Parker's voice dripped with determination.

"They won't. We're too strong for them."

"I'm not giving up on figuring out something to put them in their place though. They shouldn't even be allowed to contribute to anything charitable the way they try to backstab everyone."

"Don't worry about it, Parker. Let it go and let's just enjoy what we're doing." Tina could tell that Parker was going to keep pushing herself until she made herself sick about it.

They talked a few more minutes before they said good-bye. Tina stood up and went in search of Cole. She wanted him to call Shane or Allen and get them to watch Parker closely. They needed to distract her so she wasn't worrying so much.

She found both him and Zack in the office. They both looked up when she knocked on the door and walked in. She loved how their faces lit up when she walked in. They made her feel special no matter what was going on.

"Cole, I'm worried about Parker. She's really taking this personally. Can you call and talk to Shane and Allen? Maybe they could spend a little more time distracting her so she isn't moping about it."

"I'll do that, but I'm almost certain they are doing everything they can already. They know she's worried."

"How are you holding up, baby?" Zack walked around the desk and pulled her into his arms.

"I'm okay. Just worried about everyone."

"You look tired, baby." Cole reached out and ran a finger down her cheek. "There are circles under your eyes."

"I'm just stressed I guess. I'm sleeping okay."

"Once Christmas is over with, you're going to take it easy for a few days. I'm glad you're not working any the rest of this month." Zack kissed the top of her head.

"We'll all take it easy after this is over with. You know, if it wasn't for those kids, I'd almost be willing to call it all off. With it being kids though, I can't do it."

"We know, baby. We don't expect you to handle it all yourself. Let the others help and share the responsibility, Tina. I don't like seeing you worn out like this." Cole tapped her on the nose with his index finger.

She grinned at him and left them in the office while she headed to the kitchen. A glass of tea sounded good to her right then. Maybe an idea on how to handle those bitches would come to her while she relaxed with tea and cookies. After pouring a tall glass of iced tea and grabbing a couple of cookies, Tina walked into the den and relaxed on the couch. Propping her feet up, she sipped her tea before taking a bite out of a cookie. Dinner hadn't been that long ago, but she was still hungry. She wasn't sure what was going on, but the last few days had really drained her.

When she finished her cookies and the glass of tea, she set the empty cup on the end table and lay back against the arm of the couch. She yawned and wondered if maybe she should call the others and find out if anything was going on with them. Maybe in a little while. She closed her eyes, and the last thing she remembered was thinking that digging up some dirt on Caro and her witch hunters sounded like a good idea to her.

Chapter Ten

Brandy and Alexis hovered over Alexis's computer as they searched the information Alexis had been able to dig up on Caro and the others.

"You're a genius, Brandy. Everyone has dirt, and sometimes the ones who scream the loudest have the most dirt to hide." Alexis grinned at her accomplice.

"I figured as much. I've been poor white trash my entire life, so no one really thought much of talking in front of me or around me. I knew all the best secrets on everyone in my town."

"Well, finding out their little secrets is proving to be entertaining, especially your suggestion on finding out what happened with the women's shelter. They really fucked that up." Alexis laughed. "I bet they don't think anyone would find out about that little screwup."

"Well, I don't want to do anything that will lead to problems for the shelter. Those women need all the help they can get," Brandy said.

"We'll make sure nothing blows back on them." Alexis grinned as she continued working on the computer.

Neal walked into the office carrying a pitcher of lemonade. "Thought you might be getting thirsty with all the devious planning you two are doing there."

"Thanks, hon." Alexis pulled him down for a kiss after he set the tray on the desk.

"How's it going?"

"We've got about all we need to put a stop to their meddling. We're just tidying it all up right now." Alexis poured a glass of lemonade for Brandy then one for herself.

"Mark and I are ready to look it over whenever you finish." Neal saluted them before walking out of the office.

"What do you think Parker will think about this?" Brandy asked her.

"I think she'll be relieved that we were able to come up with something to burst their bubble." Alexis could tell that Brandy was a little uncomfortable around everyone for some reason.

At first, she thought it was that she was just shy, but the more she had gotten to know her, the more Alexis felt that Brandy didn't feel as if she fit in with them for some reason. It was almost like she thought she wasn't good enough to be a part of them. Now, after listening to her explain about being privy to all sorts of secrets because people didn't think she was of any importance to worry about, she thought that may be the case. They talked around her as if she wasn't even there. She said they didn't worry that she would spread their secrets because no one would ever believe anything she said anyway. She was from the wrong side of the tracks.

As soon as all of this was over with, Alexis was going to make sure that Brandy knew better than to think that she wasn't a part of their group as much as anyone else. The woman had a good head on her shoulders and had come up with what they needed to do to put those bitches of Caro in their place.

"Okay, let's look over it one more time, and then we'll let Mark and Neal take a look." Alexis smiled at the other woman as they waited for the papers to spit out of the printer.

"Do you think the others will be okay with it?"

"They're going to be ecstatic with what you've come up with, Brandy."

"I didn't do anything. You did all the work."

"All I did was pretty things up and make them legally safe for us. You are the one who had the idea and dug up most of the information. Talking to those women and finding out what had happened will kill two birds with one stone."

"As long as no one gets hurt, then I'm happy."

Alexis looked over the printouts with a critical eye while pondering something in her head. Brandy would make a great investigative reporter. She had a nose for a story and knew how to dig up the information that others might overlook. She would suggest it to her later.

"The only ones who are going to get hurt are Caro and her gang. Don't worry about it anymore, Brandy. We're doing the right thing."

The phone rang, but Alexis let it ring, knowing that one of her husbands would get it. A few seconds later, Neal walked in, holding the phone with a very serious expression on his face.

"Brandy, it's West."

"What's wrong?" She took the phone and repeated her question. "What's wrong?"

Neal pulled Alexis aside and whispered in her ear. "Children's services are at her house to talk to them about Matthew."

"What? Why? They take excellent care of him."

Alexis grabbed Brandy when the other woman started crying and searching for her purse. Neal helped Alexis steady the other woman. Alexis found her purse and wrapped an arm around her friend.

"We're going to drive you home. You can't drive like this."

"They're talking about taking Matthew away from me. What am I going to do?"

Alexis's heart broke for the other woman. She couldn't imagine what Brandy was feeling right then. She grabbed her jump drive and the printout and followed Brandy and Neal out of the room. She was going to call everyone to meet once the situation was taken care of. They needed to get into gear and put a stop to Caro's vicious plans.

Mark drove Brandy's car while Alexis and Neal carried the crying woman in their car. When they drove up, it was to find the entire gang already in attendance. Brandy had stopped crying and was sitting quietly in the backseat. Alexis saw West all but run down the drive to get her. He pulled open the door and took her in his arms. His nod at them said it all. He appreciated that they had brought her home safe.

"What do you need, man?" Mark asked.

"Prayer. Prayer that I don't kill that bitch." West cuddled his wife against his chest and carried her toward the house.

They followed him and piled into the den with everyone else. Brandy immediately grabbed Matthew out of Kyle's arms and held him against her breast. It was obvious that he didn't know what was going on. He smiled up at his mom with the innocence of a baby. Alexis couldn't help but smile at the picture they made with West on one side and Kyle on the other. No child could be more loved or better taken care of than little Matthew.

"What happened?" Alexis finally asked.

"We were waiting for Brandy to get here to go over it." West squeezed his wife's shoulder. "A woman from the child welfare department showed up at two this afternoon and said she was there to assess the living conditions where Matthew was living. She said someone had turned them in as unfit parents."

"That's ridiculous!" Tina's face was almost red in color.

"Easy, baby. We know there's nothing to the claim."

"What did you tell her? Why didn't you call me right away?" Brandy asked, looking down at her child.

"She wouldn't let us call until she had questioned us. We told her that someone was yanking her chain and that Matthew was well cared for." Kyle's face seemed almost made of stone.

"She looked around the house and checked out Matthew's room and our bedroom. She asked about our living arrangements. We answered all of her questions honestly. She wasn't ugly or anything. I think she was a little put out at having to check into it in the first place," West said.

"What did she say before she left?" Alexis hoped that there wouldn't be any follow-up to this.

"She said that she couldn't see where Matthew was being abused or neglected and that how we raised him was our business as long as we weren't harming him. She said she would be making a follow-up visit at some point in the next three weeks per protocol." West ran his hand lightly over his son's head.

"Brandy, she wants you to go see her in the office tomorrow. You're supposed to call her and make an appointment to go in. She said she needs to talk to the mother to complete her report."

"I can't believe this is happening." Brandy still had tears in her eyes, but she had them under control right then.

"Don't worry, baby. No one is going to take Matthew from us." West hugged her tightly against him.

"Brandy, I think it's time to tell everyone about what we found out. Those women have gone too far." Alexis held out the papers she had brought in with her.

"Tell them. I can't think right now." Brandy kept rocking back and forth on the couch with Kyle and West hugging her between them.

"What are you talking about?" Parker asked. She and her husbands were standing in the doorway.

Alexis drew in a deep breath. "Brandy figured out that Caro and the others had something to hide since they weren't sponsoring the women's shelter anymore. She went and talked to some of the people there and found out some interesting things about their support."

"You went to the shelter by yourself?" West pulled back and looked at Brandy with a frown.

"I went in the middle of the day. There wasn't any reason to worry about going by myself." Brandy's eyes were flashing.

Alexis liked that Brandy had the fire in her again. The sight of her friend looking helpless and scared had worried her. Now the life was back in her.

"Anyway, what she found out was that they raised money for the shelter the first year and handed over a check without ever visiting the place even once. The next year, they showed up to tell them how they needed to be using the money they were donating. They didn't approve of some of the programs the shelter has, such as helping women escape their abusive spouses by helping them locate a new place to live."

"Why would they object to helping them when they've been hurt like that?"

Parker spoke up. "They probably don't approve of the women in the first place because most of them come from broken homes to begin with."

"That's ridiculous," Tina all but spit out.

"They believe that they are the only ones worth anything. Everyone else is beneath them." Parker waved her hand.

"Well, that's not all. They nearly got one poor woman killed by her estranged husband. Caro and the others decided to do a little help in the counseling area and talked one young woman into giving her husband another chance despite the fact that he had put her in the hospital the month before and she'd only been out for a week. He had nearly choked her to death and broken two ribs." Alexis drew in a deep breath. This gave her the chills just thinking about it again.

"The woman was barely twenty-two and scared to death. She didn't have any family, so she didn't have anywhere to go. The counselors were setting her up with a job and a place to live in another town. Caro didn't like that they were spending the money to get her out of town. She took it on herself to talk this young woman into going back home instead. She even went so far as to contact the husband and facilitate them meeting to work things out."

"Why did they let her do that?" Briana asked.

"They counselors didn't know what was going on. If they had, they would have put a stop to it. Instead, the poor woman let Caro drive her to the restaurant where she was going to meet her husband. Instead of sticking around to be sure everything was okay, she left the woman there and went home as if nothing was wrong."

"That bitch. What happened to the young woman?" Carly's voice hitched.

"Her husband talked her into going home with him. A neighbor heard her screaming an hour later and called the police. When they got there, the woman's husband was standing over her with a knife threatening to cut her throat. He'd beaten her and stabbed her five times. He had rebroken her arm and ruptured her spleen by kicking her in the side. They had to rush her to surgery to save her life." Alexis looked around the room.

Everyone was quiet, thinking about the poor woman. Alexis was planning to find out if she was okay. If she needed help, she was going to be sure she got it. For now, though, they had to handle their own problems.

"What else do you know, Alexis?" Parker was watching closely.

"They were told that they wouldn't accept any of their donations again because of their interference. They were told not to show up at the shelter again, too. And"—Alexis looked down at her paper—"Evelyn Witherspoon refuses to do any further dinners or balls for them for fund-raising."

Parker started laughing. Evidently that was major for some reason. Alexis couldn't find out much on the old woman. The only thing she knew was that the woman had millions outside even what her husband had.

"What's so funny, Parker?" Tina cut her eyes over to Alexis.

"Evelyn is the grand dame of it all when it comes to organizing charity fund-raisers. She doesn't chair any of the committees or anything anymore, but she will sponsor others and host their parties for them. If she's cut them off, then they are really going to have to struggle to raise money. They probably were going to use the orphanage as a bargaining point with Evelyn. Evelyn was adopted as a child. They were going to try and appeal to her special love of the kids."

Alexis nodded and smiled. Knowing this made it all the better what they had planned to do. She grinned and passed their work over to Parker.

"What's this?" she asked, taking the papers.

"Read it. You'll understand."

Parker looked down at the papers in her hand and started reading. Her expression moved from surprise to disbelief before settling into smug approval. She looked up with a wide grin on her face.

"Its good, isn't it." Alexis smiled.

Parker nodded and handed it over to Tina to read. The men were all looking at them with suspicion. Alexis knew they wanted to know what they were reading. It proved that they were good men when they waited for the women to all read the papers before they got them. She smiled at Parker when Cole finished reading and passed it over to Zack with a smile on his face. Alexis was glad to see that he apparently approved.

"Parker, can you handle the logistics of it?" she asked.

"I'm all over it. I can't wait to put this in motion."

Alexis smiled at Parker's enthusiasm. Everything was going to work out like it should. All they had to do was wait and watch what happened once Parker handled the first part. Brandy looked better once she realized that everyone was in on the project. Seeing her so heartbroken and scared had been hard. Alexis wanted to take care of this problem once and for all so that when she and her husbands decided to have children, there wouldn't be any chance someone could cause problems for them.

"I'll be calling James Thornton, Sarah Beth's husband first thing in the morning to get things started. Then I think I'll call my dear stepmother and clue her in on a few things. If anyone can spread the word, it will be Elaine." Parker laughed when Shane frowned at her. "Don't worry, honey. She will never know what hit her."

"That woman needs to be horsewhipped," he said.

"Shane!" Parker laughed.

Alexis knew there was no love lost between those three and Parker's stepmother. The woman had tried to have Parker committed. Parker's husbands were very protective of her and their baby.

Everyone hugged on Brandy, giving her their support before leaving. Alexis waited until only she and Brandy were left in the room. She wanted to make sure the other woman knew that Alexis would stand by her and help keep her child safe.

"How are you doing?"

Brandy smiled and looked down at a sleeping Matthew. "I'm okay. I don't know if I'll be able to let Matthew sleep in his room tonight or not, though."

"I can understand that, and I don't blame you. We're going to take care of this, though."

"I know. Thanks, Alexis. I never had friends before like I do now. I can't believe how supportive everyone is being. Thank you."

Alexis hugged her and Matthew together. Then she walked outside to join her men where they were talking to Kyle and West. Brandy was right. Their group was the best family she'd ever had. When Neal pulled her into his arms and Mark leaned over and kissed her on the cheek, Alexis felt well and truly loved. They said good-bye to everyone, and Alexis let Kyle settle her in the car. Looking back as they drove off, Alexis watched West take Matthew out of Brandy's arms and carry him inside as West wrapped his arms around Brandy. They looked like a perfect family to her. It didn't matter that there were two husbands in the family. That just meant that there was twice the love.

Chapter Eleven

"Parker. Are you sure you want to do this?" James's worry was obvious in his voice.

"I'm sure. We've all had enough of Caro and her escapades, James. Can you do it or not?" Parker almost held her breath.

If he wouldn't help her, then she would have to look for another lawyer. It would take time and they didn't have a lot of time. They were going shopping Saturday for the children's presents and didn't want there to be any way the other women could cause trouble for them while they were out. Everything hinged on James helping them.

"Okay. I'll help."

Parker let out her breath in a loud whoosh. "Thank you so much! Tell Sarah Beth I said hi. I'll call her later."

As soon as Parker ended that call, she called the other women to clue them in on what was going on. She hoped this wouldn't somehow bite them on the ass. Brandy and Alexis had really seemed to have thought of everything. All they had to do now was to wait for the paper to come out the next day. Knowing her old crowd, they would gobble up the newspaper as soon as they were up and about. They lived off of gossip.

"You look like a cross between a cat that ate the canary and a constipated cow." Allen walked over and wrapped his arms around her.

"Allen! That wasn't nice."

He chuckled and kissed the side of her neck. "Got you smiling though. What's up?"

"I just called James about setting up the ad in the paper. I guess I'm a little anxious about it now."

Allen nodded and kissed her softly on the lips. "Relax, baby. It will be fine. You guys thought of everything. Besides, they deserve it."

"I can't help worrying that it will backfire on us. All we wanted was for them to leave us alone." Parker sighed and fiddled with the neckline of Allen's shirt.

"So stop feeling guilty about it. They started it and you're ending it. Let's go find Shane and Addison and go out for lunch."

Parker smiled and followed Allen back into the kitchen where Shane had Addison in her high chair playing with a baby book while he straightened up the kitchen.

"What's up, guys?" he asked.

"Thought we would go out for lunch today. Parker is antsy about the newspaper ad she and the girls set up." Allen hugged her against him.

"Sounds like a good idea. I'll go get Addy's bag. Why don't you call and see if anyone wants to meet us somewhere?" Shane ran a hand over Addison's head and walked across the kitchen toward the den.

Allen pulled out his phone and began calling folks while Parker disengaged Addison form the high chair. Five minutes later, they were ready to climb into the car. Allen secured Addy in her car seat then slid in next to her in the backseat. Shane helped Parker in before closing the door after her and walking around to the driver's side to take his place.

"Who all is coming?" Parker asked.

"I got Cole and Neal. They were going to spread the word to the others, so I'm not sure. We might even have everyone."

When they pulled up outside the restaurant ten minutes later, Cole, Zack, Tina, Kyle, West, and Brandy along with their son Matthew were already there. As Parker and Allen got Addison out of her car seat, Ranger, Drew, and Carly drove up. Parker began to feel better with everyone showing up.

By the time they were settled in the back room of the restaurant, everyone else had arrived. They were taking up the entire back room and all of the available high chairs. The waitress was one of the regulars at the place, so she was used to dealing with them. She quickly got their drink orders and made sure they had everything else they needed.

"What's up, Parker?" Tina asked.

"I guess I'm feeling a little nervous about the newspaper article now. James is drawing it up so that it can't be used against us, and it should be in tomorrow's paper."

"I can't wait to read it!" Briana grinned. "They deserve every word and more."

"I agree, but I can't help but be worried about it. They've threatened our children. You just don't do that." Parker huffed out a breath.

"Which is why they deserve what they get," Brandy fumed.

"Brandy hasn't put poor Matthew down for anything except to change him since that social worker was there." West looked just as angry as Brandy.

"They knew better than to try to accuse you of anything with Addison," Cole began. "So they went after Brandy because she appears vulnerable. She works part time as a waitress sometimes or doesn't work at all. They thought they were picking the weakest link."

"We showed them, though." Briana smiled and grabbed the saltshaker out of Darla's hands. Deanna made a swipe at the pepper, but Dillon was too fast for her.

The waitress returned with their drinks and took their food orders. They jumped from one idea to the next all during the meal. Parker noticed that neither Tina nor Carly were eating much. Mostly they were playing with their food. She hoped they weren't coming down with something right at Christmas. Plus, they had the big shopping day on Saturday. It would take all of them working together to get everything on the list.

It had been decided that the men would handle the kids while they were out on Saturday. Now she wondered if maybe a couple of them shouldn't come along for support. They could be their pack mules if nothing else. She grinned to herself and listened as Briana talked about how the twins where getting into everything.

After everyone had finished their meal, they gathered outside in the parking lot and made plans for that Saturday. She warned everyone about the newspaper article coming out the next day and that it would probably be a good idea to stay close to home if they could. She knew that Carly and Alexis were both going into work. Carly had been lucky so far that her bosses hadn't fired her over the stunt Caro and her crew had pulled.

By the time they had made it back home, Parker was exhausted and decided she needed a nap along with Addison. Shane and Allen chuckled and helped her put Addison down for her nap.

"I think we could all use a little downtime," Allen said.

Shane began pulling off Parker's clothes while Allen shucked his in record time.

"Something tells me sleep isn't all you have on your minds." Parker smiled up at Shane.

"Well, Allen and I are always ready for anything that comes up."

Parker couldn't help but laugh when Shane's cock jumped up out of his jeans when he unfastened them.

"See, we're always ready for you, baby." Allen grasped his dick in his hand and pumped it a few times.

"I thought we were going to take a nap, guys." Parker pretended to pout.

"Oh, we'll get to that." Shane backed her up until the back of her legs hit the edge of the bed.

Parker bounced when she fell back on the bed. Shane followed her down and took her mouth in a searing kiss. His lips burned hers until she opened her mouth for his tongue. He slid alongside hers and then teased her until she was moaning.

"Move over, Shane. I want her pussy. I can already taste her sweetness on my tongue." Allen separated her legs and settled between them.

The first swipe of his tongue across her pussy lips tore a scream from her that Shane quickly caught in his mouth. They were in a mood, she could tell. She was glad that baby Addison could sleep through anything.

* * * *

Carly climbed out of the truck and followed her men into the house. She hadn't had much of an appetite at lunch. It wasn't that the food hadn't been good. It was that she wasn't really feeling well. She hoped she wasn't getting sick right at Christmas. There was too much to get done. Between shopping for the kids at the orphanage and wrapping all the gifts, there was all the cooking to get done as well.

Right then, it all sounded like too much to her. What was wrong with her? Normally she had more energy than even the guys.

"Babe, you look a little pale. Are you okay?" Drew pulled her into his arms and kissed her forehead after rubbing his cheek against it.

"I'm fine. Just a little tired. I think I'll take a nap."

"I'll help you get settled." Drew took her hand and towed her through the house and up the stairs to the bedroom.

Ranger called up the stairs. "I'll be up later. I want to finish in the office."

Carly let Drew undress her and help her settle in bed under the covers. Then he stripped and joined her. He pulled her back into his arms and she quickly fell asleep that way.

When she opened her eyes sometime later, it was to find herself cocooned between both of her men. Drew's hand was on her breast and Ranger's was cupping her pussy. It was how she normally woke up when they were both in the bed with her. It made her feel safe and loved.

She wasn't sure how long she had been asleep, but she felt much better. In fact, she felt great. The soft snores of her men made her smile. Maybe she would play a little bit now that she was awake.

Carly shifted a little in the bed and managed to get her hands on both men's cocks. She slowly pumped them until they grew hard and were helping her in her efforts to arouse them. She knew they were awake by now since they were lifting their hips as they shoved their dicks between her fists.

"Baby, you're killing us." Drew's tight voice made her smile.

She loved driving them crazy. When they got to the point that they couldn't take it any longer, they would attack her, and she loved it. Ranger was so intense that if you didn't know him better, you might think he was dangerous. She knew better though. He would never hurt her. She knew it would kill something inside of him to cause her any harm or distress.

"I need in that hot ass, babe. Are you going to let me have it?" Ranger's growl turned her on.

"Depends on if you're good or not. Are you a good boy, Ranger?"

"You know I'm not, Carly. I'm never a good boy." Ranger's deep, guttural words plucked at her nerves deep inside her cunt.

Carly was counting on him being a very bad boy. It was when he was at his best.

"Show me, Ranger. Make me yours."

Drew chuckled and pulled away to lie back on the bed as Ranger grabbed Carly by her waist and turned her over so that she was on all fours kneeling on the bed. She looked over at Drew and winked at him. She couldn't wait for Ranger to take her. He knew exactly how to get her ready and then blow her mind.

"You want me in that hot ass, don't you, Carly?"

"Only if you can fill me up, Ranger. Can you do that?"

Ranger growled and spread her legs wider before pulling her ass cheeks apart as well. He licked her there, paying extra attention to her puckered opening. He swiped his tongue across it making her draw in a deep breath. Then he pulled back, and she knew he was reaching for the lube. She wiggled her ass in hopes he would hurry up.

"Stop shaking your ass, baby. I'm going to spank it if you don't be still." She could tell Ranger was grinning.

A cold drop of lube hit her back hole then his finger was pressing inward, smoothing the lube inside of her as it pushed deeper. At first there was only some pressure, but when he added the second finger, a small bite of pain reminded her of how full she was going to be in a few minutes. Ranger slowly pumped two fingers in and out of her ass, adding more lube as he did. The pain soon morphed into need as her nerve endings came alive and made her itch for something more.

"Please, Ranger. I need you inside of me."

"I don't want to hurt you, Carly. Let me get you ready first."

Carly wasn't sure she could stand waiting much longer. Her body was on fire with need. She moaned and pushed back against his fingers as he added a third. She hissed out a loud *yes* and dropped her head as he stretched her back hole.

"Drew. She's ready. Hurry up, man. I'm already so close I might not make it inside her." Ranger's voice gave away how aroused he was.

Drew moved under Carly until he was able to line up his hard cock with her slit. He grabbed her hip with one hand and held his dick steady with the other as he plunged upward inside of her. She groaned deep in her throat at the fullness of his shaft inside her cunt with Ranger's fingers pressing deep into her ass. She couldn't wait for Ranger to replace his fingers with his thick cock. She knew they would burn her alive.

Drew thrust upward inside of her over and over until he was as deep as he could go. Then he stopped and pulled her down to his chest, holding her there with his hands across her back so that Ranger could enter her rear while she was being held still.

"Fuck, she's tight, Ranger. Hurry up, man." Drew's voice cracked as she squeezed down around him. He popped her on the ass.

"What was that for?" she asked.

"Be still and stop squeezing my dick until Ranger gets inside of that tight ass of yours. I'm not coming before I even get to fuck you."

Carly smiled with her face pressed against Drew's shoulder. She loved being able to make them lose control. Right now it wasn't to her advantage, so she would be good for now. The men would be on edge, and if she pushed them, they would come too soon. She was hoping for a nice long ride.

Ranger removed his fingers before squeezing a fresh line of lube along her ass. Then the spongy head of his cock pressed into her dark rosette. The pressure was almost more than she could bear at first, but once his cockhead pushed through, the pain morphed into pleasure as his long thick shaft filled her back end. In one strong push, he managed to bury himself balls deep inside of her. She couldn't stop the low keening noise she made as he pressed against the thin membrane separating him and Drew's cocks from each other.

Carly was almost certain she could feel them in her throat. They didn't move. Their heavy panting above and below her let her know that they were trying to regain control and cool off their need to come before moving again. She tried to be still as well, but with all the pressure and the overwhelming fullness she felt, she couldn't handle it for long. Finally, she pulled off of Drew, pressing back against Ranger then dropped hard on the cock in her pussy and pulled off of the one in her ass.

"Fuck! Carly. Your ass is hot as sin."

She squeezed down on both men and smiled at their creative curses in her ears.

"Move! I need you to move or I'm going to scream."

Her men took her at her word and began to move in tandem, their rhythm so perfect it was as if they had choreographed it. She flowed between them as they took turns filling her body then retreating and leaving one area of her achingly empty while filling the other one with their hot hard cocks.

"Aw, God! I'm not going to last. She's too fucking tight." Ranger's strained confession thrilled her.

"More! Fuck me harder."

They groaned together and began to power in and out of her tight holes. Carly sobbed out her release as their combined efforts shot her off like a bottle rocket on the Fourth of July. She felt as if her insides were on fire as she keened out their names. Her pussy tightened around Drew as her ass squeezed Ranger's dick.

Seconds later, her men climaxed filling her body with their hot cum. It sent another shiver down her spine as she fought to breathe around the fullness of having them inside of her. Nothing could ever compare to having her men surrounding her, filling her. It made her feel complete and a part of them at the same time.

Despite having just awakened from a nap, Carly was exhausted and closed her eyes for just a second, or maybe longer.

Chapter Twelve

Alexis answered the phone in her office on the second ring. For some reason, she felt like it was important.

"Hello?"

"It's started." Parker's strained voice wasn't surprising. It was nearly nine, so most people would be reading their paper by now.

"What happened?"

"Caro called, threatening to sue. I explained that she couldn't sue if it was the truth."

"What did she say to that?" Alexis couldn't stop the grin that spread across her face.

"Well, outside of the swear words, I'm not really sure. It didn't make a whole lot of sense." Parker seemed to relax some with that statement.

"Any other phone calls yet?"

"Not yet. It's still early."

"Keep me informed. I'm going to be here all day since I want to have more time off during Christmas. Are we still meeting at Tina's Saturday morning to go shopping?" Alexis was getting excited.

"So far. Nothing has been said, yet. I'll let you know." Parker hung up the phone, leaving Alexis smiling.

"Alexis. What is this I'm reading in the paper this morning?" Vernon Eddison walked into her office with the paper opened to the article they had sponsored.

"I'm not sure, Mr. Eddison. What is it about?" Inside, she cringed. She had hoped he wouldn't put two and two together.

"Well it would seem that your friends are waging a war against another charity out there. What do you know about it? Hmm?" he asked.

"Well, it's like this, Sir. We pledged to adopt the Dallas Children's Home for Christmas and began making plans and setting up our charity drive when another group challenged us. They tried to nose us out of the picture and accused us of some pretty nasty things. They even called Child Protective Services on one of us. So we fought back." She spread out her arms and shrugged.

"I see. So everything in this article is true. You have proof of it. 'Cause if it isn't or you don't have proof, they can sue you, Alexis. I can tell you drew this up."

"Oh, we have proof. We also hired a lawyer to handle the proof and approve the verbiage of the article."

"I'm a little miffed that you didn't ask us to handle this for you," Vernon said.

Alexis hadn't counted on that. She really didn't think they would make the connection since they weren't really all that friendly in the first place. Though she enjoyed working part time for them, she hadn't felt as close to them as she had to her previous bosses. She'd chalked it up to the job not being as important to her as it once was.

"I'm sorry, sir. I really didn't think you would want to be a part of it. It's really sort of juvenile, but we had to fight fire with fire."

"Yes, I'm sure you did. Next time don't write us off when you have something going on like this. Not only does it reflect back on us, but we might want to be a part of it outside of buying tickets to a raffle." He grinned at her and turned and walked back into his office.

Alexis was surprised at his attitude and decided that she needed to be sure they knew how much she did enjoy working for them. Her career just wasn't her priority anymore. Neal and Mark were.

She pulled out her copy of the newspaper and read over the article once again. The brief introduction talked about the overwhelming need for charities in the Dallas area, naming many of the worthy causes as well as some of the groups who were regular sponsors of some of them. Then it discussed the charities that were usually picked up around holidays like Christmas and Thanksgiving.

The article went on to list some of the generous contributions to those charities over the years before settling into the reason for the article in the first place, the feud between The Dirty Dozen and Caro's group, aptly named The Drama Queens. By the time she finished reading, Alexis was grinning from ear to ear. It had turned out even better than she would have imagined. Parker's lawyer friend had tweaked a few words to keep it completely legal while dragging Caro's cause through the mud.

There was no way they would be able to dig their way out of this. Besides, where was their threat now that they had pretty much announced their lifestyle to the world? They had armed themselves using freedom of sexual orientation among other things while touting the importance of family values in caring for those less fortunate.

The crème de la crème was where Caro's selfishness had nearly cost a young woman her life and had gotten her banned from having anything to do with the women's shelter. How could a group run a charity when they were banned from them? Since the women's shelter wasn't the only black mark on their record, the article seemed less like a blatant attack on Caro's Divas and more like an exposé on one group's inability to handle themselves or the charity work they said they wanted to provide.

All in all, Alexis felt like it was a roaring success. Now all they had to do was step back and wait to see what happened next. She prayed there wouldn't be any bad publicity for The Dirty Dozen out of it. She felt as if they had been backed into a corner. To jump out fighting was the only option open to them.

Her phone rang again. She checked caller ID and recognized Tina's number.

"Hey, Tina. What do you think?"

"It turned out perfect! Cole was impressed." Tina's voice held enough excitement for all of them.

Alexis chuckled. "Have you heard from anyone yet?"

"No not yet. I expect it will be Parker who will get the phone calls, though. She'll keep us informed."

They chatted for a few more minutes then hung up when Alexis's phone began to buzz with incoming calls. For the next hour she fielded calls for her bosses with an occasional call from her friends. Parker called her at lunchtime to fill her in on what was going on.

"Caro called me not long after I got off the phone with you. She was fit to be tied to say the least. She had calmed down some from the original phone call, so not every word was a curse word."

"What did she have to say this time?" Alexis asked.

"She said they would leave us alone as long as we stayed out of their business from then on. I informed her that we were never in her business until she opened her big mouth and spewed pure bull crap at us."

Parker chuckled then continued. "She said they would handle charity for the hospital and the schools and stay away from the women's shelter and the Dallas Children's Home. She was snarky about that saying that she had informed everyone that we were handling those two charities from now on. I'm sure she thinks we can't deal with two by ourselves. I just told her fine that we would take care of them."

"That does put a little more pressure on us for Christmas since we hadn't planned on the added responsibility of the shelter." Alexis frowned. They hadn't planned on that.

"I know, but we can do it. It might not be what we would have wanted, but it will be better than what they got last year. That's for damn sure." Parker's resolve was catching. Alexis vowed to do her best as well.

"What's next, Parker?"

"We meet at Tina's in the morning to go shopping. We'll have to spend the entire day to get everything we need and then wrap on

Sunday and Monday if need be. I'm sure the guys will help us all they can."

Alexis was sure she was right. After hanging up, she mulled it all over in her head for a few minutes then knocked on her boss's door. They had wanted to help. Well now they could.

* * * *

Briana finished updating the group's website and sighed. She hoped the added information and link to the article in the newspaper would generate some last minute donations for The Women's Shelter. Everyone had agreed to add some additional personal money into the pot and both Alexis and Carly had been able to worm added donations from their bosses. She inhaled and nearly groaned at the wonderful smell of chili that wafted across her nose. Dillon was cooking dinner. She couldn't wait.

She found Gavin entertaining the twins in the den with stuffed animals. Seeing him play with the girls always brought a lump to her throat. He was so intense and stiff looking to most people, but she saw the real man behind the facade. Gavin was tender and giving as well as handsome and strong. It was no wonder that she fell in love with him as well as his twin brother. As alike as they were, they were unique in so many ways.

She smiled and wrapped her arms around Gavin's waist. He dropped one hand onto hers and snagged a stuffed horse with the other that Darla had thrown down. The girls looked at each other and smiled before looking up at them.

"They're plotting again," Gavin said, amusement in his voice.

"Not much we can do about it. They know they have us over a barrel. We can't refuse them anything they want." Briana kissed her husband on the cheek then scooped a unicorn off the couch before she sat down and pulled Deanna into her lap.

"What are you two little angels up to now?"

Deanna just blew bubbles and grinned as if saying she'd never tell. Gavin picked up Darla and carried her over to his lounge chair to sit back and relax. The girls didn't like being apart. They both held out their hands and yelled.

Briana laughed and stood up. "See, they get what they want no matter what." She carried Deanna over to Gavin's recliner and stood there looking down at them. Deanna leaned over trying to get to her sister. Darla reached up out of Gavin's arms trying to reach Deanna. They each held their little girl so that they couldn't get to each other until they were wiggling too much to hold on to them. Brianna chuckled and gave up. She lowered her little girl into Gavin's lap and let him deal with the two monsters. She shook her head at Gavin's expression. He was obviously wrapped around the girls' little fingers. They could do no wrong, and he wasn't going to tell them no for anything.

She walked into the kitchen to find Dillon stirring the chili. "Umm, that smells wonderful. When do we eat?"

Dillon looked over his shoulder at her and held up a spoon for her to try the chili.

"Be careful. It's hot, baby."

Briana blew on the spoon and its contents before sipping a small amount of the chili into her mouth. It tasted just right.

"Perfect as always."

"It will be ready in another twenty minutes. I've got cornbread in the oven cooking now. What are the girls doing? I heard them yell out a minute ago." Dillon checked the cornbread in the oven.

"They're both in Gavin's lap. We separated them for a few minutes and they didn't like it one bit."

He chuckled. "You do realize they are going to double-team us every chance they get."

"I know. I really dread when they start trying to get us confused over who is who. I'm going to have to count on you two helping me there. I'm sure you did it to your parents all the time." Briana sat down at the island and propped her chin in her hands.

"Yeah, our parents, our teachers, the girls we dated." He waggled his eyebrows.

"I knew I married a couple of pranksters. Seriously, though. If they couldn't tell the difference between you, they deserved it. It's so obvious to me."

"Only to you, baby. No one else was ever able to tell us apart. Mom could if given enough time, but not our dads. They just punished us both no matter whose fault it actually was."

"I'm sure you both deserved it anyway." She giggled when he kissed her nose.

"Did you get the website updated like you wanted?" Dillon asked.

"Yep. Let's hope it works and we get some more donations. We all want to go down to the shelter tomorrow morning on our way to go shopping to see what they really need the most."

Dillon frowned. "I'm not sure that's such a good idea, baby."

"Cole and Zack are going with us anyway. We won't be alone."

Dillon let out a breath. She knew he felt better knowing there would be a man or two with them. The shelter wasn't in the best part of Dallas. Even at eight in the morning, it wouldn't be the safest place for a group of women. When Tina had suggested it, Cole and Zack had immediately volunteered to go with them. When Tina had informed them that they could help carry packages, too, the two men had rolled their eyes and groaned.

"We'll keep the girls happy while you're gone. Kyle and West talked about bringing Matthew over as well."

"I bet if you called Shane and Allen they would bring Addison over. Then you would have plenty of help with the girls." Briana grinned.

"Good idea. I'll call them after dinner. Go help Gavin with the girls. I'll have the high chairs at the table ready."

They all worked together to settle the twins into their seats and feed them before settling down to their own meals. Once they had finished, Briana helped Dillon bathe the girls while Gavin did the dishes. Then they met up in the den to watch TV before bed. Two hours later, they climbed the stairs to head to bed. The three of them decided on a shower, but it was obvious to Briana that the guys weren't intent on getting clean. As soon as she stepped into the spray, they began to kiss and suck on her breasts. She couldn't help but giggle when Gavin lost suction on the nipple he had when Dillon turned her to face him.

"Hey, man. I was busy."

"My turn. You had her so that the water was pounding me in the face."

They knelt before her and kissed and licked their way across her chest and each latched on to a nipple. They nipped and pulled on them until she was moaning with need. Gavin slipped a finger between her pussy lips and teased her clit. She couldn't help pressing her pelvis into him to increase the pressure of his finger there.

"You're soaking wet, baby. Dillon, I'm going to taste her. Keep her busy for me so she doesn't strangle me."

Dillon chuckled and grabbed her hands in his before returning to play with her nipples. The feel of his mouth there as he tweaked her nipple with his tongue had chills spreading along her spine. When Gavin's tongue touched her clit, she nearly screamed. Then he was lapping at her pussy lips like a puppy.

"You taste like spicy honey, babe. I can't get enough of you."

"Well hurry up because I'm next." Dillon growled at his brother.

"Don't stop, guys. Please. I'm already so close." She couldn't believe how wound up her body had been already. It was almost as if she'd already had an hour's worth of foreplay before they started touching her.

Sometimes the mind was the sexiest organ. She'd been thinking about how she wanted them the entire time she'd been working on the webpage. For some reason she found that she was excessively horny.

Gavin stabbed her pussy with his stiffened tongue and fucked her with it while he squeezed his fingers into her ass cheeks. Dillon was pulling and twisting her nipples as he claimed her mouth. Then, as if having already planned it, the two men switched spots, and Dillon took over teasing her clit with his tongue and stabbing her pussy with his fingers. Gavin sucked and nipped at her neck as he flicked her nipples with his fingers.

She groaned then yelled out when Dillon thrust two fingers deep in her cunt. She rolled her pelvis toward him and wrapped her arms around Gavin, pressing her hardened nipples into his chest. She rubbed against him. If they didn't fill her pussy with their hard cocks soon, she was going to lose it.

"Let's dry off and move to the bed, Gavin. There's more room there."

Gavin stepped away from her and grabbed towels for them. Once they were dried off, Dillon picked her up and carried her to the bedroom. He set her on the edge of the bed while Gavin checked the baby monitor to be sure it was on.

"Get on your hands and knees, baby." Gavin popped her ass lightly when she complied.

Dillon knelt on the bed in front of her and held his cock toward her mouth. She licked her lips, making him moan. Then she ran her tongue across the dripping slit to taste the pre-cum that had gathered there. Dillon's hiss was music to her ears. She loved knowing she could affect them like that.

Gavin rubbed the head of his cock up and down her slit before pressing inward until her pussy opened for him. He fucked in and out of her several times until he made it all the way against her cervix. Briana could feel the weight of his balls against her pussy lips. Then he began moving inside of her, and it took all of her concentration to focus on Dillon's thick dick sliding in and out of her mouth. He tasted tangy, making her mouth water even more as she wrapped her tongue around his shaft.

"Fuck, your mouth is like a hot oven, baby." Dillon moaned when she took him to the back of her throat and swallowed around him. His strangled cry was music to her ears.

Gavin began powering into her with his thick shaft, filling her cunt and tapping her cervix with each thrust. The pleasure/pain ramped up her arousal until she wasn't sure she would last much longer. Already it felt like her toes were curling as the two men gave her all they had.

Dillon's fingers in her scalp as she swallowed his dick sent another round of chills down her spine. Her orgasm was building on the edge of her periphery, warning her of what was to come. She thought every time with her men was the best that it could be, only to be proven wrong the next time. She couldn't get enough of their loving and wanted to please them more than she wanted her next breath.

She gently rolled Dillon's balls in her hand before pressing against the thin tissue just below his anus. Then she ran her finger, wet with her saliva around his back hole, applying just a little pressure. It was all it took for him to spew in her mouth. His cum filled her mouth and throat as she hummed around him.

Even as his fingers dug into her scalp, Gavin began to lose his rhythm as he tunneled in and out of her wet pussy. He reached around and pressed a finger against her clit, sending her flying into ecstasy as he pumped his cock inside of her cunt twice more before filling her womb with his cum. The hot streams splashing against her cervix sent another wave of pleasure throughout her body. Briana collapsed to the bed with her ass in the air held tightly in Gavin's hands.

Long seconds later, the three of them cuddled together under the covers. Briana could hear her men's snores on either side of her. Over that was the sound of the twin's cooing to each other. She smiled. Nothing was better than this. Looking over at the clock, she smiled and closed her eyes. Tomorrow would be a challenge for all of them. She needed to get some sleep in preparation.

Chapter Thirteen

Tina listened as everyone talked about the upcoming shopping trip. Everyone had gathered at her house by seven that morning. She looked over where Zack and Cole were standing by the door with amused expressions on their faces. No doubt those looks would soon change to ones of exasperation by the end of the day.

They were going to take three cars so there would be plenty of room for all of the purchases. Each car was in charge of a list with needed gifts. They would split up and fill their lists then meet at lunch to compare notes and see where everyone was. To begin with, they were all going to the women's shelter to meet the managers and find out what was needed the most.

Ranger was going to go in one car while Zack and Cole took the other two cars. That way there would be one man with each group of women. It was for safety and they could carry more bags. The men were going to be bored out of their minds before the day was done, Tina was sure, but she thought it was a good idea anyway.

"Everyone ready to go?" Cole finally called out.

The general consensus was that they were. He nodded and led the way outside to the vehicles. Everyone divided up and climbed into their assigned car. Tina, Carly, and Zack paired up and took the lead. The other two cars fell into line behind them as they made their way to downtown Dallas and the women's shelter.

When they arrived, it was to find that there were eleven women in residence with a total of fifteen children. They were literally wall-to-wall children. With school out, they had nowhere to go. It just about broke Tina's heart to see them all looking both angry and scared at the same time. The women appeared almost hopeless, and it was bleeding over into their children.

They crowded into the manager's office and talked about what was needed most and what they hoped for the future. Clothes and food were the number-one items. They especially needed nice clothes that would be suitable for job interviews for the women. Finding a job and then a place to live were their objectives to starting a new life. The manager provided them with a list of sizes and needs.

Their group spent nearly an hour there talking and visiting with the occupants as well as with Jill, one of the managers. Tina had a headful of ideas by the time they left and couldn't wait until they gathered again to discuss them. She was sure the others would have some as well.

She divided the list from the shelter with the other two groups before they headed out to shop. It would take a lot of work to gather everything needed on their respective lists. They had a budget for each group, and meeting it was going to be difficult. Tina and Carly started with clothes, planning to work their way to toys. She doubted they would make it that far before lunch anyway.

"What do you think about these, Tina?" Carly held up a bag of socks for young boys. "There are six pairs in each bag."

"Good idea. Let's get four bags. That should cover everyone on both of our lists." Tina crossed boys' socks off of the list.

"I'm so glad that the newspaper article got those women to back off. I just hope we don't have any more trouble." Carly dropped the socks into the shopping cart.

"I know what you mean, but I'm happy regardless. Seeing Brandy so devastated broke my heart. I thought Cole and Zack were going to have heart attacks."

"Well, I am glad we ended up with the women's shelter, too. They obviously need a lot of help, and they weren't getting it from anyone."

Tina smiled. Carly was right. There was so much potential there for improvements that she couldn't wait to get started. The guys were going to fuss about her plans to renovate the shelter, but they would eventually fall into line. There was no way they would turn their backs on what was needed. She was sure of it.

They spent the next three hours shopping for clothes and personal necessities for their portion of the group. Tina got very excited when they found a sale on dresses that would be perfect for so many of the women at the shelter. Before it was over with, they managed to finish over half of their list before lunch.

Zack finally called a halt to their shopping at noon and escorted them back to the car with their bags. They met up with the others at a restaurant halfway between the three groups. When they descended on the poor waitress at the height of the lunch hour, Tina almost felt sorry for her. The young woman moved some tables together and settled them in with menus and their drink orders.

"How is it going so far, everyone?" Tina sipped her tea and listened to the shopping stories.

"We've gotten most of ours done already!" Alexis grinned across the table at her.

"We're doing pretty good ourselves," she said. "We got lucky and found some dresses on sale that are perfect for the shelter."

"We found a sale on jeans and managed to get everyone a pair." Briana was looking over their list.

"Did y'all notice that they didn't have any cabinets or storage anywhere at the shelter? I bet the guys could solve that easily enough," Brandy said.

"I was thinking about that, too. I thought once we get this out of the way, we would talk to the guys about it." Tina was glad someone else thought about it.

"What are you going to talk to the guys about later?" Cole asked, speaking up over the noise.

"We'll talk to you later, honey. There's too much going on right now." Tina hoped he wouldn't push it right then. She wanted time to plot her plea with them.

Parker winked at her from the other side of the table. She knew what she was up to. Between the two of them, they would come up with the perfect project and arguments to support it. All they had to do was get through Christmas and New Year's Eve. Then they could approach the men with their proposal to overhaul the women's shelter.

They chatted over lunch and then separated again to finish up their shopping. They all agreed to meet up at Tina's house by six that night to organize everything for wrapping on Sunday. Cole kept telling them there wouldn't be enough room for everything at their place, but Tina ignored him. She was sure there would be plenty of room if they divided up the gifts by age groups and assigned different ones to different rooms.

Four hours later, Carly yawned as they carried the last of their purchases to the car. Poor Zack had his arms full leaving several bags for each of them to carry as well.

"Do you think we got everything?" Carly asked.

Tina grinned over the stack of boxes in her arms. "According to my list we did."

"I'm ready to put my feet up. I don't think I've ever shopped this hard in my life."

"Hey, shopping is hard work." Tina grinned at Carly when Zack groaned.

"You two are slave drivers. My arms are never going to be the same again," Zack complained.

"Poor baby. I'll give you a massage later."

"Promise?"

Tina chuckled and handed over her boxes when he opened the trunk. "I promise."

"I wonder if I can get Drew or Ranger to massage my feet for me when we get home." Carly held out her bags to Zack before climbing in the backseat.

"I'm sure they'll be more than happy to play with your feet." Tina closed the car door after getting in the front passenger side.

"Don't give Tina any ideas, Carly. She'll expect us to take care of her feet next."

"Of course you will, honey." Tina looked over her shoulder at Carly.

"See. What did I tell you?" Zack started the car and pulled out of the parking spot into traffic.

"Wow! We might have finished at a decent hour, but getting home is going to take some time." Tina pulled her list out of her pocket and started looking over it again.

She still couldn't believe they had managed to finish so soon. She honestly thought it might even take an additional day to get everything. She hoped everyone else had been able to finish as well. That would put them ahead of schedule in getting everything wrapped and delivered. Tina was all for that. She couldn't wait to talk to Parker about it. She thought about calling her on the cell phone, but decided to wait until they were all together. Besides, she had a headache and felt a little dizzy. Maybe a short nap was in order.

* * * *

Alexis started to help unload the cars until the men put a stop to it. She rolled her eyes with the other women and hurried inside where it was much warmer. The men never let them do anything that might be considered hard. They all treated the women like spoiled queens. She didn't think she would actually be complaining anytime soon.

Shrugging out of her coat, she realized that she hadn't had that much fun in years. Wrapping the gifts was going to be even better.

She couldn't wait to get started. This was going to be the best Christmas ever.

As she walked into the kitchen, she realized she was feeling a little weak.

Maybe a snack would be a good idea.

She looked for Tina and found her directing traffic as the men brought in their bags of gifts.

"Tina, do you mind if I fix something to eat. I'm feeling a little weak." Alexis noticed that Tina appeared pale.

Maybe I'm not the only one who isn't feeling so hot.

"That sounds like a great idea." She turned around and called out to Carly. "Carly, help Alexis make some snacks for us while we organize this mess. I think we could all use something to eat."

Carly nodded and hurried into the kitchen with Alexis. The other woman grinned and fanned herself.

"I was getting hot out there. As cold as it is outside, something's got to be wrong with me."

Alexis laughed. "I was feeling a little weak. I think I'm starved. Let's see what we have to work with."

They worked together for the next twenty minutes putting together sandwiches, cheese, and crackers. Alexis nibbled some as they set everything on the table so anyone who wanted something could stop by and grab what they wanted. Carly made coffee and distributed mugs to everyone who wanted it.

Durn. I wonder if something is going around? Carly's face is all flushed and Tina is pale looking. Maybe we picked something up while we were out shopping.

"How are you girls holding up in here?" Neal and Drew walked in as they were washing up.

"All through. The food is out on the table. Is everything situated out there now?" Alexis snuggled up against Neal's chest as he wrapped his arms around her.

"I think Tina and Parker have it under control. You're shaking, baby. What's wrong?" Neal pulled back to look at her.

"I think I got a little too hungry before I got something to eat. I'm fine. Let's go tell everyone the food is ready."

"Don't think you have to announce it," Drew said as they walked into the dining room. "I think everyone already found it."

Alexis and Carly chuckled at the crowd around the table. Alexis accepted a paper plate with cheese and crackers from Mark. He lifted a brow when she started to hand it back, so she nibbled from it.

Once everyone had stuffed their faces, Parker divided them all up once again into groups so that each room with gifts would have at least two people to wrap gifts with two people in charge of watching the children. Alexis and Carly worked on wrapping gifts for girls under the age of twelve. She had to admit, it was fun but a lot of work to keep everything straight. At least they had names for their gifts. Some of the gifts were just for *boys* or *girls*.

By the time everyone had finished wrapping, it was almost midnight. Alexis was almost asleep on her feet. She'd already called Ranger into the office where they had been wrapping to get Carly. The poor woman had fallen asleep standing up and nearly hit the floor before Alexis got to her. She couldn't help but worry that there was something going on. She hesitated to bring it up when it might be nothing.

Alexis sighed and finished straightening up the wrapping paper that was left and stacked the presents out of the way. Mark and Neal walked in and shook their head.

"You're not any better off than Carly was when Ranger carried her out to the car." Neal picked her up.

Alexis was too tired to even squeal when he did. "I think we're all pretty much exhausted."

"I don't like how pale you are, baby. Let's get you home." Mark bent over and kissed her before Neal carried her out of the room.

"Hey, Alexis, are you okay?" Tina took her hand and squeezed it.

"I'm fine. These guys like carrying me around. It comes in handy when I'm feeling lazy."

Tina laughed then took a step back and her eyes rolled back in her head. Alexis yelled out her name, but it was too late. Shane made a grab for her and managed to keep her from hitting her head on the coffee table. Then Cole and Zack elbowed their way through and picked her up.

"Neal, put me down so I can check on Tina." Alexis was afraid something was seriously wrong.

"Cole and Zack have her. Let's get out of the way and give them some room." Neal carried her over toward the door.

Everyone was talking at once. Parker brought a wet dish cloth to Cole and suggested they put her to bed. Alexis hoped she was just worn out like the rest of them. It had been a long, exhausting day for everyone.

"She's coming around. We'll take care of her. You can all go home and we'll talk tomorrow." Zack helped Cole pick her up. "We'll call if anything happens."

Shane and Allen helped straighten everything up while Parker saw to the leftover food. Alexis felt terrible for not helping put it away, but Parker assured her that she could handle it.

"I'll talk to you tomorrow. Go on and get some rest, Alexis. You're dead on your feet, too."

"Ha! I'm not on my feet." Alexis tried to add some humor to the situation. "I'm on Neal's feet."

"Go home, Alexis. You're not even making sense now." Parker grinned and shooed her off.

As they drove toward home, she closed her eyes and fell asleep. Never even knowing when they made it. The last thing on her mind was worry over Tina. She had been looking a little ill for the last two days. She hoped she wouldn't be sick for Christmas.

Chapter Fourteen

Christmas Eve afternoon, everyone gathered at the shelter with the gifts they were bringing. Jill, one of the managers, met them at the door when they arrived. She was as excited as if the gifts were for her. Parker grinned as she teared up over their generosity.

"You have no idea how much this will mean to the women here. I can't wait for them to open them. Thank you all." Jill wiped her eyes and hugged each of the women.

"We have one more surprise." Tina spoke up this time.

Cole helped her open up a sketch pad to show Jill the plans to renovate the shelter one room at a time over the next six months.

"You don't have any storage at all here. We're going to add shelves all along this wall and a long closet here for all the clothes." Cole pointed out the various areas where they were going to improve the room.

"How? We can't afford all of this right now. Our budget is already approved for next year." Jill shook her head.

"You don't have to worry about a thing. The supplies are being donated from various businesses, and thanks to Brandy, our website guru, we have a *gift* account where people are sending in money and other donations to help fund the renovations." Zack pointed out Brandy.

Jill started crying all over again. The women in the shelter who had been staying hidden slowly came out to see what was wrong with their friend. She finally managed to explain to them that there was nothing wrong. Instead, she handed them packages to open for the shelter. As each gift was unwrapped, the women began to smile. The children took the toys and played quietly in the back of the large common room while their moms saw hope in the new clothes and household items for the first time since they had arrived.

"You can't imagine what this is to them," Jill said. "You've given them more than a dress to wear to an interview or a set of silverware for when they find their own place. You've given them a taste of hope that they will survive this. Thank you from the bottom of my heart."

Parker could only smile because there was such a lump in her throat at the moment that she knew she couldn't speak. All the charity balls and dinners in the world could never equal this moment for her. Actually seeing and being a part of this meant more to her than anything. How could anyone not become involved and feel the need to personally help these people?

Caro and her group didn't deserve to be a part of something like this. They didn't appreciate what they had much less understand what it was like to have nothing. Maybe Parker didn't know what it was like to go without, but she understood what it meant to give freely from her heart and receive freely the love that they returned.

She hugged each of the women and children before they left. Thank God for the chance to help them and thank Him for Brandy's website. None of them had expected the depth of generosity that people showed who had visited the site over the last few days. Brandy had managed to garner the needed attention for their charities through pictures and prose. They were very lucky to have her.

They loaded back up in the cars and headed toward the Dallas Children's Home with the rest of their gifts. Parker and Tina held hands the entire time they rode. There was no need to say anything. They both knew what the other was thinking.

When they arrived, she noticed that everyone was holding hands as they waited for the men to unload the presents and carry them into the common area of the building. The staff had all of the children waiting in another part of the house while they arranged the presents under the tree. As much as they all wanted to be a part of the actual celebration when they opened their gifts, they had agreed that it was best that the children wait until the next morning to open them.

Instead, once everything was situated, they were going to share cookies and punch with the children. Parker could hardly wait. Addison, along with Darla, Deanna, and Matthew were at Tina's with a couple of babysitters so that they all could be a part of this. They had all worked hard to bring these children some joy when they had no parents of their own. It was only right that they all celebrate together.

One of the women spoke up. "Are you all ready for the kids?"

"Bring them on." Gavin and Dillon looked as excited as Parker felt.

The woman opened the door to the back and called out. In less than five seconds, boys and girls of all ages ran through the door and headed right for the Christmas tree. It was obvious that they all wanted to tear into the gifts, but they were careful not to disturb them much. They pointed and called out to each other when they found their name on a tag.

"Look at them. They are so excited." Parker couldn't keep the tears from her eyes as she squeezed Tina's hand.

"Look at the little girl with the black hair. Isn't she adorable?" Tina pointed out a child of about seven who was holding an older boy's hand. She seemed to be afraid to get too close to the tree. The teenage boy was trying to urge her closer.

Tina let go of Parker's hand and walked over to the two of them. She crouched in front of the little girl and spoke to her. Then she looked up at the boy and nodded before holding out her hand to the little girl. Parker prayed that Tina, Cole, and Zack would be able to have children one day. Tina was so good with them.

Tina managed to get the little girl to sit in her lap next to the tree and look at the lights and the gifts. The boy stood behind them with his hands in the pockets of his jeans. Cole and Zack walked over to him and started talking to him. Parker smiled and turned to join Shane and Allen in the middle of a group of kids around ten or twelve years old. They were talking about what they had asked Santa for. Shane had a little boy on his lap and Allen had two little girls in his. Parker plopped down in the middle of them to share in the joy.

Nearly two hours later, Parker gathered with everyone to say good-bye to the kids. She hated to leave, but they needed naps before dinner that night and she wanted to get home to Addison. She needed to hug her little girl and be sure she knew how much she was loved. Being with this many children so hungry for love had reminded her how lucky she was to have had her parents for as long as she did and how blessed she was to have Shane and Allen and little Addison.

Tina wrapped her arms around Parker and squeezed when they were out by the cars again.

"What's that for?" she asked.

Tina giggled. "We're going to take Antonio and his sister, Rachel home after Christmas for a week."

"Those where the two children you were spending time with?" Parker asked.

"Yep. They are so cute. Antonio is so protective of his little sister. The only way they have been able to find a home for her was without him, but it didn't work out because Rachel cried and refused to eat when they took her from him."

"That is so sad. Poor thing. I'm sure Antonio was hurting without her, too." Parker couldn't imagine being separated from the only family she had left after losing her parents.

"He was, but he wanted her to have a chance at a normal home. We're going to have fun with them." Tina's smile was contagious.

"How old is Antonio?"

"He's fourteen."

"Everyone ready to head back to the house?" Cole asked.

There were excited murmurs all over as they all piled into their vehicles to return to Cole, Zack, and Tina's place. They were going to watch Christmas movies and visit each other for a few hours. Parker grinned as her men bundled her into the car. Christmas Eve wasn't over yet.

* * * *

Zack watched as Tina waved at the last of their guests. He was worried about her. She'd been feeling bad for over a week now, and after passing out the other day, he and Cole were keeping a close watch on her. She looked so pale and fragile, which wasn't like their Tina at all.

"How are you feeling, babe?" Zack wrapped his arms around her as Cole closed the door.

"Tired, but happy. This was one of the most wonderful days of my life. Thank you both so much!" Tears shone in her eyes.

Cole kissed her as Zack held her in his arms. He knew they were tears of happiness, but he didn't like seeing them anyway. He didn't want to ever see her cry. He wanted her to only know joy and happiness. He and Cole had talked about how she'd been really anxious over getting pregnant and wondering if maybe that was what was wrong. Maybe she was worrying over it too much and making herself sick. That was why they had agreed to bring the children home with them for a week after Christmas. If she was happy and relaxed around them, she wouldn't be so anxious about getting pregnant right away.

Zack sighed. At least he hoped that would work. He and Cole both liked the two children. Antonio was a young man in a child's body. He'd been caring for his sister for nearly three years now. Zack could sense the young boy's anxiety over keeping her safe and making her happy. It wasn't all that different from the way he and Cole strived to take care of Tina.

"Ready for bed?" Cole asked, looking at their wife.

Tina smiled. "Let me finish cleaning up the kitchen, and I'll be right up."

"We'll help you so it won't take very long." Zack nipped at her shoulder before releasing his hold on her.

He and Cole followed her into the kitchen to wipe down the counters and put away the drying dishes. They teased Tina about what they had gotten her for Christmas, reminding her that she couldn't open it until the next morning.

"I'm going to sneak down here before you wake up in the morning and unwrap all my gifts first." She laughed when Cole growled at her.

"I'll spank that pretty ass of yours if you do." Zack quickly took a step back when she lunged at him with the dish towel.

"Hey! No fair popping me." Zack grinned.

Cole stacked plates in the cabinet as Tina hip checked him. She handed him more plates to put up.

"What do you think about little Rachel and Antonio, guys? Aren't they sweet?"

Cole winked at Zack. "Antonio seems to really care about his sister. Brothers don't always act like that."

"He knows she's scared. He's trying to make her feel safe." Tina dried off a glass and handed it over to Zack.

"Rachel seemed to trust you. She was sitting in your lap before we left," Zack said.

"It broke my heart to see her so afraid of getting too close to the Christmas tree. She was afraid that she would get into trouble if she got too close."

"I wonder why?" Cole closed the cabinet door and folded his arms as he leaned against the cabinets.

"I don't know. I didn't want to ask too many questions."

Zack took Tina's hand and kissed her knuckles. "She's going to be a different little girl once you've spent some time with her. Cole and I will spend time with Antonio and do guy stuff with him."

"Thanks. I want to spend as much time with her as I can. I want to spend time with him, too, but he will benefit more from time with you two than with me." Tina leaned into Zack then moved over to Cole. "Thank you both for letting me bring them here next week."

"We're going to enjoy it as much as you will, baby." Cole kissed her before pulling her into his arms. "Let's head up to bed now. You need to get some sleep."

Zack watched as Tina grinned and pulled away from Cole to run out of the kitchen toward the den. They looked at each other then chased after her.

Just as they entered the den, Zack's heart dropped when he saw Tina collapse halfway up the stairs and fall backward. He and Cole raced to reach her before she hit her head. Cole managed to grab her as her head hit the bottom step.

"Fuck! Tina, baby." He pulled her into his arms.

Zack grabbed her hand, holding it to his chest. "Is she okay?"

"She's not waking up. She's breathing."

"Is her head bleeding?"

Cole held her to his chest. "Look and see. I can't feel anything."

Zack leaned over and checked, but he didn't see anything. "Doesn't look like it. We need to take her to the hospital. This is the second time she's passed out. Something's wrong."

"You drive." Cole lifted her in his arms as he stood up.

Zack grabbed the keys to the car and hurried to open the doors for Cole. Once he had them settled in the car, he locked up the house and jumped in the car to drive. She was going to be okay. There wasn't another option. He couldn't survive if she wasn't in their lives. She made his world turn and brought the sunshine every morning.

Chapter Fifteen

"Why didn't you call us and tell us you were sick?" Alexis asked. She felt terrible that they hadn't known and been there to help Tina.

"There was nothing any of you could have done. I'm fine now." Tina's beaming smile belied that she had been sick at all.

Alexis was excited and had news to share, but she didn't want to be insensitive. Maybe she would tell everyone later. Right now, they were all busy helping Tina get ready for the kids from the children's home that would be visiting over the next week. The guys were putting up a basketball goal despite the temperatures being in the twenties outside.

"Do you think the bedroom will be comfortable enough for them? I thought that Antonio would want his own room, but Cole is probably right. He'll feel better having Rachel in the same room since they don't really know us that well." Tina was flitting around the room, straightening pillows and tightening the covers on the twin beds.

Alexis grinned. "I'm sure it will be perfect for them. They are so lucky that you are going to let them visit for a week. Are you sure you're well enough to handle two kids right now?"

"I'm fine. Besides, I have Cole and Zack to help me. They won't be any trouble at all."

Parker chuckled and held up a book from the bookshelf. "I remember this book. My dad used to read it to me. I had forgotten all about it. I need to get one for Addison."

Carly ran her hand down the center of one of the twin beds. Alexis thought she seemed awfully quiet. Since she was smiling, she didn't think there was anything wrong. Maybe Alexis was just projecting her good news on everyone else.

"I think everything is ready, Tina. Let's go check on the guys." Briana grabbed Tina's hand and pulled her out of the room. "I don't trust Kyle and Dillon not to be teaching the girls something they don't need to know."

Brandy giggled. "Tell me about it. Matthew is already winking at all the girls."

"You know he's going to be such a flirt with dads like those two," Briana said.

"Just wait until your girls grow up and want to date," Brandy pointed out. "I bet you anything your husbands are going to be standing at the door with shotguns."

Parker nodded her head in agreement. Alexis was sure Brandy was right. The men wouldn't be able to help themselves when their daughters grew up. Right now they had everything under control, but come high school, those days were going to be a distant memory.

They located the men all congregated in the den with the children watching a sports channel. Alexis smiled as both Cole and Zack jumped up to pull Tina between them. It was obvious they were being extra careful of her. She smiled when Neal and Mark crooked their finger toward her. They had huge grins on their faces as well.

Zack grabbed the remote off the coffee table and muted the sound on the TV as everyone found a seat in the den. Allen pulled Addison on his lap while Dillon and Gavin had a daughter apiece. Brandy and Matthew were sitting on West's lap and Carly, Drew, and Roger all sat on the floor on cushions in front of the couch.

"When are you picking up the kids, Cole?" Shane asked.

"We'll get them tomorrow morning after breakfast and keep them until Sunday afternoon around two or three. They have to be back in time to get settled to return to school."

"We were hoping that maybe you would all come over on Saturday for a party for them. We planned to cook out hot dogs and hamburgers on the grill and watch kid-friendly movies," Zack added.

"They would enjoy being around everyone and the other kids, too." Tina looked hopeful.

"Sounds like a great idea to me." Alexis squeezed Mark's hand.

"We'll be there," Shane added.

Everyone talked about what they would bring and added their ideas for what Cole, Zack, and Tina could do during the week with the children while they had them. Alexis loved being a part of the gang. It was like one big happy family. They all cared about each other and supported them no matter what.

"Hey, everyone!" Tina stood up, holding the hands of her men. "We've got something to tell you."

Alexis turned her attention from playing with Matthew and looked at Tina and her husbands. They all looked pretty excited.

"The reason I was sick the other night was Cole and Zack's fault."

"Hey!" Zack pulled her hair before kissing her.

Everyone grew silent wondering what she was talking about. Alexis held Neal's hand and felt Mark's on her shoulder.

"It seems that despite all our best attempts to prevent it," Tina began. "I'm going to have a baby."

Alexis started laughing and jumped up to hug Tina. She couldn't get close enough with Parker, Brandy, and Briana beating her. She and Carly just looked at each other and laughed. Then all of the women started crying together.

"Hey! What's with the tears?" Cole demanded.

Shane and Allen just shook their heads. "Get used to it, man. When they're pregnant they cry all the time."

"They're not all pregnant, are they?" Zack asked.

"God, I hope not!" Gavin wrapped his arms around Briana's waist and pulled her away from Tina.

"Actually," Carly began. "I am." Drew and Ranger grinned like idiots.

"Well, I guess if we're spilling the beans, then I should confess that I am, too." Alexis couldn't hold it in any longer. Everyone began talking and crying all over again.

"Can you believe it? We're all going to have babies at the same time!" Tina jumped up and down until Cole put a stop to it.

"Easy, baby. You're going to jiggle poor junior until he's seasick."

"I'm going to have a little girl. You watch and see." Tina wiped at her eyes as she smiled up at him.

Alexis was so excited that her friends were having babies, too. She knew how much Tina had wanted to get pregnant and how worried she'd been. Now that she was, maybe she would relax more and lose some of the stress that had seemed to be plaguing her lately. Of course, Cole and Zack would be riding her hard to take it easy from now on. She was already getting some of that from her men.

"Tina, what about Antonio and Rachel? Are you sure having them next week isn't going to be too much for you?" Parker asked.

"Not at all. I'm fine now that we know what is going on. I was a little anemic, so the vitamins will help with that. There's no way I'm going to cancel their visit."

"Well, if you need help, you can always call on us to help," Brandy said.

"I know. You're all the best family I've ever had." Tina started crying again, and the men all moaned.

"Don't start that again, babe." Zack brushed a tear away with his thumb. "I can't stand to see you cry."

Cole looked over at Zack and shook his head. "Might as well admit it, man. We're going to adopt those kids anyway. Looks like we're having triplets, guys."

Tina squealed and threw herself in Cole's arms. Alexis couldn't stop the tears from falling. There had been too much happening in all of their lives lately for her to keep from boohooing along with everyone else.

Mark kissed her lightly on the lips before passing her to Neal for another kiss. She loved her men. They had helped her learn to relax and enjoy life instead of trying to make her life into something she thought she wanted. Now they were going to have a little baby to love and adore. If anyone would have asked her even a year ago if she planned to have children she wouldn't have been able to answer them. She'd never thought she was the mothering type until she met her men and the rest of The Dirty Dozen crew.

Now all she could think about was how happy she was and how much she loved all her friends. Between her part-time job, her husbands, her baby on the way, and the charity work they were doing as a group, Alexis figured she had a pretty full life. In fact, it was overflowing with happiness. Looking ahead, she saw baby showers, first steps, and first days at school along with a whole lot of Dirty Dozen Happiness.

THE END

WWW.MARLAMONROE.COM

ABOUT THE AUTHOR

Marla Monroe has been writing professionally for about ten years now. Her first book with Siren was published in January of 2011. She loves to write and spends every spare minute either at the keyboard or reading another Siren author. She writes everything from sizzling-hot contemporary cowboys to science-fiction ménages with the occasional badass biker thrown in for good measure.

Marla lives in the Southern US and works full time at a busy hospital. When not writing, she loves to travel, spend time with her cats, and read. She's always eager to try something new and especially enjoys the research for her books.

She loves to hear from readers about what they are looking for next. You can reach Marla at themarlamonroe@yahoo.com or visit her website at www.marlamonroe.com.

For all titles by Marla Monroe, please visit
www.bookstrand.com/marla-monroe

Siren Publishing, Inc.
www.SirenPublishing.com

Lightning Source UK Ltd.
Milton Keynes UK
UKHW011015051118
331793UK00013B/1435/P

9 781622 425341